CHARLIE'S PROMISE

"I won't let anything happen to you," Charlie said.

"Because I'm your friend or because . . . ?"

His gaze dropped again to Lila's mouth before flipping back up. "Because one lazy day out on a hammock, I handed you my heart, and I don't think I ever got it back."

And with those words went the last of his control, his need to have her closer to him greater than his need to appease his friend.

His mouth came down on hers, and suddenly he no longer cared about anything, not Lucas, not himself, only this moment. A surge of emotions hit him all at once—confusion and happiness, guilt and relief, each more conflicting than the last, but one thing was 100 percent clear: She was kissing him back. And that single thing meant there was no turning back. If she wanted him, he was there.

Books by Melissa West

Hamilton Stables
RACING HEARTS
WILD HEARTS
SILENT HEARTS

The Littleton Brothers
FIGHTING LOVE
CHASING LOVE

Published by Kensington Publishing Corporation

CHASING LOVE

Melissa West

LYRICAL SHINE
Kensington Publishing Corp.
www.kensingtonbooks.com

LYRICAL SHINE BOOKS are published by

Kensington Publishing Corp.
119 West 40th Street
New York, NY 10018

All Kensington titles, imprints, and distributed lines are available at special quantity discounts for bulk purchases for sales promotion, premiums, fund-raising, educational, or institutional use.

Special book excerpts or customized printings can also be created to fit specific needs. For details, write or phone the office of the Kensington Sales Manager: Kensington Publishing Corp., 119 West 40th Street, New York, NY 10018. Attn. Sales Department. Phone: 1-800-221-2647.

Lyrical Shine and Lyrical Shine logo Reg. U.S. Pat. & TM Off.

First Electronic Edition: May 2017
eISBN-13: 978-1-60183-990-9
eISBN-10: 1-60183-990-1

First Print Edition: May 2017
ISBN-13: 978-1-60183-991-6
ISBN-10: 1-60183-991-X

Printed in the United States of America

ACKNOWLEDGMENTS

Many thanks to God and to my family for supporting and guiding me daily.

Thank you so much to the staff at Kensington/Lyrical, including John, Rebecca, Michelle, and everyone who helped this book from beginning to end. You are all so wonderful!

Thanks to all my author friends, namely Rachel Harris and Cindi Madsen, for keeping me sane.

I couldn't write without the support of my readers and the many amazing bloggers and book reviewers out there. Thank you so much for doing what you do and taking a chance on my stories!

Chapter One

"Nah-ah, boy, you better take that dog on out of here."

Charlie Littleton tightened his hold on Henry's leash and shot Patty a look. "You know he doesn't bark."

The bakery owner placed a hand on her hip and cocked it for effect. Like always, she wore an apron with the AJ&P Bakery yellow-and-blue logo on it, though you could scarcely see it through the flour and spices smeared across the apron.

"Right," Patty said now. "A dog that don't bark. Is that sort of like a man who don't eat? Because as far as I'm concerned that's a fictional being. Like the dog. But if you do find a man who will share his sandwich, you be sure to point him in my direction, okay? But seeing as how that man don't exist, kind of like that nonbarking dog don't exist, I don't expect you to be introducing me to him anytime soon." She winked at him and clucked her tongue. "Now, you take that cute bottom of yours out of here, leave the dog in your truck, then come back and I'll make you a roast beef with extra au jus."

Charlie peered around the bakery, the smells of fresh baked bread and toasted hot sandwiches hitting his nose. His stomach grumbled. Of course, the small bakery and sandwich shop was packed today, half the town there to witness Charlie getting put in his place. A part of him wanted to remind Patty that his family's farm supplied most of her produce and could just as easily refuse to deliver, but he'd learned long ago to retreat slowly and carefully when dealing with the bakery owner.

"Fine, but I'm holding you to that extra au jus."

Patty flashed him a grin. "It'll be waiting for you, honey." Then she waved her hand through the air in a sign that he better get moving, and then she went to greet someone else. Someone without a dog.

Resigned, Charlie pushed out of the glass door and eyed his old Husky. "Sorry, boy. I'll bring you some leftovers, though." He unlocked his Silverado, cranked the truck, and rolled down the windows. It was a mild sixty out in Crestler's Key, Kentucky, a perfect early spring day, but Henry meant more to him than most of the people in the town, and if he was going to be forced to stay in Charlie's truck, then he'd do it with a nice breeze.

With a long glance down Main Street at the row of shops—Southern Dive, his family's sports and outdoors shop at the very end—Charlie couldn't help wondering if he was making the right decisions in his life.

He'd moved back to Crestler's Key after living in the Florida Keys for five years. There, he'd operated a small scuba diving business, his life as much under water as above it. And he loved every moment of it. Then there were the women, too many to count, always around, always eager to occupy a little bit of his time. He'd been content with that life, never asking for more and never wanting it. He was a typical twenty-something and enjoyed every bit of his young age.

Then he met Jade, and hell if he didn't fall hook, line, and sinker.

Still to this day, years later, he remembered with painful clarity her walking down the dock at the marina and stopping outside his houseboat, long sun-bleached blond hair and even longer legs. She was beautiful in that natural, God-made way—his kryptonite, when it came to women, so all it took was one look and he was gone.

It took mere days, maybe even hours, for her to rope him into her world. She had innocence behind that beauty that he couldn't refuse, and weeks passed with them tangled in each other's arms, a new kind of happiness swirling in Charlie's chest. She would never fill the spot someone else had once filled, someone he was never allowed to care for, someone he told himself he could—would—forget, but Jade made him feel good. They meshed together perfectly, peanut butter and freaking jelly.

Until that fateful day when he woke to discover she'd taken everything he owned. His dog. His wallet, which she used to drain his checking account. His prized possessions. Even the coin collection his grandfather had left him. Every. Single. Thing. Hell, if he hadn't been on the houseboat, he felt sure she'd have sailed off with it, too.

And while, yeah, the money thing sucked, and the coin collection sucked even more, what really dropped him into the depression bucket was losing his old dog, Rocky.

He'd rescued Rocky as a puppy from the pound, more mutt than anything, and with a broken left leg. Thousands of dollars in vet bills later, and that dog was his only friend down there. And his idiotic self had let some vixen walk in and steal him.

The thought brought on a fresh wave of guilt, and he contemplated going to talk to Patty again, convince her that they could sit out on the back patio, but then he'd been through this argument with her before. Besides, this was Crestler's Key, not Florida, and he knew everyone in town. No one would take his dog.

Still, just to be safe, he hit the locks on his truck twice, before heading back into AJ&P, determined to rehash this with Patty before he left if she hoped to continue to get discounted produce from the farm.

"There you are, cute bottom."

Ah, crap.

Grimacing, Charlie pivoted to find his best friend, Lucas, already seated at one of the white-washed wooden tables, a giant smirk on his face. "Funny," Charlie said. "You know, I was excited to see you and then you had to go and open that big mouth." The men laughed, then hugged, because it'd been too damn long.

They took their seats and Lucas joked, "Thought you were going to cry there when she said you couldn't bring Henry in here."

Charlie peeked out the window at his truck before returning his gaze to his friend. "Well, she ought to remember who's supplying all her produce."

"So you're going to hold her produce ransom until she lets you bring in your dog? Dude, you need a chick in your life. Stat."

Charlie laughed, until he glanced around and noticed several of the women he'd dated off and on eating at the bakery, half of them glaring at him. "Yeah . . . think I'll pass on that one. Thanks, though."

"What's the deal with your insane overprotectiveness of Henry anyway? He's a giant dog. He can take care of himself."

Yeah, well, Rocky had been a big dog, too, and that didn't save him from that thieving witch of a woman. Charlie had searched for the dog for nearly a year, all to no avail. Jade was probably halfway across the world now, with his money and his coin collection and his dog. Damn woman. No, damn *women*. They were more trouble than they would ever be worth.

Lucas continued to stare at him with a questioning look, but all Charlie could say was the same excuse he always said. Because no one, not Lucas, not his brothers Zac or Brady, no one knew about Jade or what she'd done to him. The humiliation would be too much.

"Henry had a rough childhood. Gotta protect the boy now."

"Right . . ."

MaryAnn, one of AJ&P's waitresses, came over then to get their order, and Lucas smiled a little too wide at his former high-school flame before clearing his throat and trying for mock-cool. Charlie suppressed a grin. MaryAnn, with her wavy blond hair and deep brown eyes, still looked exactly as she did in high school. And just like in high school, she was still 100 percent in love with Lucas. "Hey, there," MaryAnn said, matching his smile. "I didn't know you were home."

Lucas shrugged. "Three-day leave before going back."

"When is your tour over?" she asked, her eyes filling with a bit of hope that she probably wished wasn't there. She and Lucas had mutually ended their relationship when she realized he intended to be a career soldier, and having lost her brother in Iraq, she said she couldn't live that life. It was a mature decision, they had both said, but now ten years later, they both still looked like they regretted it. And come to think of it, Charlie couldn't remember a single woman Lucas had dated seriously since ending things with MaryAnn.

With another careful glance at his old girlfriend, Lucas relaxed into his chair, the single thing between them now back front and center. "Three months, then I'll have a few weeks off, before another one."

MaryAnn nodded slowly, and then flipped her attention over to Charlie for the first time, like she couldn't bear to look at Lucas another second. "Your regular?"

"Yeah, though Patty promised extra au jus if I left Henry in the truck."

"What's up with you and that dog?"

Lucas laughed. "Didn't you know? He's married to that dog. Papers and all."

"Again, funny."

Both MaryAnn and Lucas laughed, until they made eye contact

with each other and both went mum. She took their order and sauntered off, her shoulders drooped a little, and Charlie couldn't stand it
anymore.

"Seriously?"

"What?" Lucas asked.

Charlie deadpanned. "What? Are you freaking kidding me? The
whole town could feel that tension. Why not try?"

Lucas took a drink of his sweet tea, set it down, then did it
again, like he wasn't ready to speak yet. Or maybe he didn't know
what to say. "She made her intentions clear years ago. Her mind's
not changing."

"She's older now. Y'all were teenagers then. Maybe she wants
you to make the first move."

"Says the dude who hasn't been on a real date since . . ." Lucas
cocked his head. "Come to think of it, I don't think you've ever been
on a real date."

"Whatever. I date."

"Sure you do," Lucas said, relaxing now that the spotlight wasn't
on him. "You sound just like Lila, always deflecting."

And just like that, just the mention of her name, and Charlie sat
up taller, eager to hear anything that might have to do with Lucas's
little sister. "What's up with Lila these days? Still in vet school?" He
thought of Lucas's only sister, two years younger and forever tag-
ging along with the two boys when they were kids. She'd always
been pretty in a sweet, natural way, her smile and laugh infectious.
Charlie looked after her when Lucas left for basic, but then Charlie
moved to the Keys and Lila moved away to college, and he hadn't
seen her since.

"Actually she finished school. Went to work in Charlotte for a
while, but she moved back to town a week ago." He took another
drink of his tea, his look distant now, and Charlie got the distinct impression that Lucas was keeping something from him.

"Why'd she move back to town?" Charlie asked. He wondered
what Lila looked like now, if she'd kept her black hair cropped short
like she had when she was little. But then most women changed their
hair all the time, so it could be long now—beautiful. She probably
had men waiting in lines to get her attention, that bright smile of hers
forever turning the eye of everyone she passed. It had certainly caught
his eye.

Lucas shrugged. "Work stuff."

MaryAnn returned then with their food, saving Lucas from explaining, but something was definitely going on. Still, it wasn't Charlie's business, and he was never one to pry.

"She ever marry?" All right, so maybe he was one to pry.

"Nah, not her thing."

Charlie perked up at the thought, his heart light—*happy*. Wow, Lila wasn't married. He'd expected her to be—

But before he could finish the thought, Lucas pointed at him. "Don't even think about it."

Charlie threw up his hands. "Think about what?"

"Lila. And you. You and Lila."

A sarcastic laugh broke from his lips, despite the uneasiness in his chest. "You go insane again? This is me. She's like a little sister to me."

Lucas settled in his chair again, but his face was still tense. "Right . . . just like the last time. My thoughts on this haven't changed."

Cringing, Charlie thought of that fateful day in high school when he'd asked Lucas about his sister. It was a simple question—Is Lila around? Three words, nothing more. He and Lucas had always been best friends, but somewhere along the way, Charlie started noticing Lila more and more. Curious where she was, how she was doing. But needless to say, the conversation with his friend didn't go well. Lucas went ballistic, shouting all the reasons Charlie wasn't to touch his sister, and their friendship meant enough to him that he didn't.

"Relax, man. I'm not going after your sister."

Besides, Lila was the furthest thing from Charlie's type now. He wasn't into doctors or the professional type. Lucas had nothing to worry about. Nothing. But still, he couldn't deny that he was curious what adult Lila looked like and whether she would remember the time they'd almost . . .

No, surely not.

Even if he would never forget.

Lila Jacobs sat in her new Honda Pilot, which wasn't new at all, because while she was the new vet at Crestler's Key Animal Hospital, she had not received her first check, which was bound to be super-laughable anyway.

Kind of like her agreeing to work with Dr. Baxter, the town's sole vet and the grumpiest man on the planet.

She pressed her head to the steering wheel and tried to remember that she was awesome. Intelligent. Driven. Kind. Occasionally funny. She was more than capable of walking into Crestler's Key Animal Hospital and helping Dr. Baxter, a giant smile on her face the entire time. Even though he was paying her half what she could make elsewhere. And even though during the interview he kept reminding her that she was his assistant. Assistant. "Not the doctor; that's me," he had said. It took all her strength not to point out that she too was a doctor, despite the assistant title he'd given her. Not that there was anything wrong with an assistant. Assistants were great, tremendously valuable people. But she wasn't one of them. Surely, she had clarified that point, told him she would assist him with patients, but not be his admin assistant, right?

Uh oh.

Come to think of it, Lila couldn't remember exactly what they'd gone over during the interview, and now she feared what she had agreed to in her excitement to get a new job far, far away from Charlotte. Finding a job in her hometown couldn't have been more perfect. She'd see her brother when he was home, her old friends, and maybe someone else, someone who likely would still look at her like a little sister.

The thought made Lila's already nervous stomach rumble.

One thing at a time, and for now, she needed to get out of her SUV and walk into Dr. Baxter's office, assistant or not, and show that she wasn't the same little girl who used to run after her brother and Charlie.

"Deep breath, deep breath."

Lila glanced in the rearview mirror to check her makeup, which consisted of no more than mascara and lipgloss—well, tinted Chapstick, but that was something.

She reached for her work tote when a knock on her window caused her to jump back. A memory slipped into her mind, but before it could take shape, she shook her head and pushed it away. This was Crestler's Key, after all, her home. Not the city, where shadows chased you and it was hard to walk anywhere without looking over your shoulder. But then it hadn't always been that way, only after . . .

No. I won't think about that anymore.

Another knock, softer this time, had her rolling down the window to find the front-desk manager, Tracy, standing outside her door.

"Hi, Tracy," she said. "Did you need something?"

Tracy wore a turquoise blue T-shirt with the Crestler's Key Animal Hospital logo on the front left pocket—an outline of a kitten on one side of the words, a puppy on the other—and white capris. Like always, she was smiling.

"Hey there, honey. Saw you out here and didn't know if you were waiting on something or what. But you do know that you don't need a key to come on inside, right? At least not at this hour." The older lady released a loud laugh as though she'd said something especially funny, causing Lila to release her own loud laugh, though it sounded less like a laugh and more like a cackle. Both women went silent.

"Right, sorry. I was just reading over a few things." Lila motioned around her, where not a single piece of paper, brochure, or pamphlet could be found. She frowned. Damn inability to lie. Even at twenty-eight Lila still couldn't lie without fearing her mother was somewhere around, all too ready to pop her hand with a ruler.

"All right then. We'll just be inside if you need us for anything. Take all the time you need. Doc Baxter isn't back yet, anyway."

"Really? Where is he?" Lila asked, this new piece of information giving her a bit of confidence. It wasn't that Dr. Baxter was a mean man. He wasn't mean . . . exactly. He was simply old and very, very set in his ways. And a little on the anal side. Okay, a lot on the anal side. Which meant he would expect Lila to do things his way, and only his way, and the problem with that was that Lila had previously worked with a very new-age, advanced vet in Charlotte, who loved to test new things and loved to give their staff opportunities to learn and grow.

Lila suspected Dr. Baxter would be offended if she suggested trying anything outside the norm.

"He's down at Littleton Farm, checking on a new calf there."

"Did you say Littleton Farm?" Lila fumbled with her phone, dropping it between the driver's seat and center console. She groaned. Why did everything always have to fall in that exact spot, where even her small hands couldn't fit? Now she'd have to spend the next ten minutes moving the seat forward and back until she could reach the stupid phone.

With no other choice, she pressed the button for the seat and slowly and painfully it moved back. Lila reached under the seat, but couldn't feel it. So she switched to moving the seat up, this time causing the engine in the seat to whine rebelliously. Once again, though, she couldn't reach the phone.

"Ugh!"

Tracy's brow furrowed. "Are you okay? You look a little feverish."

Right, feverish. So not only did her mind react in crazy ways to hearing the Littleton name, but her body reacted as well. Thank God Tracy hadn't mentioned Charlie's name outright or Lila might lose all ability to function. She needed to pull herself together and call him or stop by or something. Rip off the seeing-him-again bandage so she could function in town without fear of running into him.

But instead of saying any of that, she waved her hand through the air casually. "Oh, no. I'm fine. Just a little hot. I'm ready to go on in if you are."

Once again, Tracy's face scrunched up. "All right."

"Got it!" Lila pulled her phone out from under her seat and grinned at Tracy, who simply stared back. All right then.

Clearing her throat, Lila turned off her SUV, grabbed her tote, and followed Tracy into the animal hospital.

It had changed from the last time she was there. On the outside, it was still an old house, converted into a business, complete with a wide front porch and decorative shutters. A black, white, and brown basset hound lay flat as a pancake outside the front door, snoring.

Tracy shook her head as she opened the door. "That's Old Babe, Baxter's dog, and I swear he sleeps more than he breathes."

Lila laughed and bent down to scratch his head, but he didn't budge an inch. "Seems sweet."

Tracy held the door and Lila stepped inside the animal hospital, her insides swirling with excitement as she peered around. The outside might be the same, but the inside had been fully renovated. The maple hardwood floors she remembered had been replaced with dark tile, and the walls were now a light tan. To the left was a small waiting area with a brown couch and two chairs. A coffee table sat between the couch and chairs, and a dozen or so animal magazines were organized on top of the table.

To the right of the door were shelves of grooming supplies—

shampoos, conditioners, brushes, trimmers, etc. Then various supplements and vitamins and over-the-counter medications, like flea-and-tick treatments. And then below all of that were stacks of organic dog and cat food.

Even in the common area, you could smell the perfumed scents coming from the grooming area, and Lila wondered if she would forever smell like a freshly-groomed poodle now or if the scent would wash away. The last office she'd worked at didn't have grooming services in the same building, so it was never something to consider.

The phone rang from the front desk before them, and Tracy sped up to catch it. "Crestler's Key Animal Hospital, this is Tracy. How may I help you?"

Lila grinned at the annoyed look that crossed the office manager's face and knew without having to ask that Baxter had called.

"Yes, she's here now, actually. Yes. Right. Of course. I'll show her now. Of course. Right, right. Sure. Anything else?" Tracy rolled her eyes and Lila had to bite her lip to keep from laughing out loud. "Okay. See you soon, bye." She hung up the phone and spun to face Lila. "I better get you set up. He'll be here in fifteen and he wants you to sit in with him on an annual check."

"But I—"

Tracy shook her head. "I know. I'm sure this is going to be as painful as watching water freeze in early winter, but trust me, it's best to just go along with it. He'll settle down soon enough."

"It's fine. Really."

Tracy smiled. "We'll see if you're this agreeable after the day is over." She released a laugh, then waved Lila on. "Come on, let me show you around."

They toured the main common area, then each of the patient rooms, then the small break room, before stopping at an office with windows along the back that overlooked the small lake behind the animal hospital. A flock of ducks milled by the water's edge, and Lila smiled as she took a step forward. "Wow, this is so nice. Thank you."

"Oh, no. That's not your office. That's Dr. Baxter's office. This one is yours." Tracy pushed open a door across from the pretty office to reveal a space so small it must have been a closet. Surely, it wasn't her office. But then she caught the grimace on Tracy's face. "I'd say what I'm thinking right now, but some say Baxter has cameras watching us, so all I'll say is that at least you can close the door if he's really driving you crazy."

Fantastic.

The phone rang again, and Lila waved for Tracy to go on. "I'm good here. I'll just set down my things."

"All right, honey."

Tracy sauntered off to grab the call, and Lila had just set down her tote on the small metal desk and tested out the small, black swivel chair, when a back door opened and it was like a storm had flown into the building.

"Lila. Lila, you in here?"

Lila jumped up and stepped outside of her office-closet to find Dr. Baxter with his hands on his hips, a trail of sweat dripping down the side of his wrinkled face. His hair had long since turned white, and that forever scowl of his had created a deep indentation in the space between his eyebrows. He was easily twenty pounds heavier than he had been the last time she saw him.

"I came here to pick up a few things, but there's been an emergency down at the Carlisle farm. A mare is delivering, but that foal of hers is turned and it's a mess. Can you wait here for me to return?"

Tracy appeared then before Lila could speak up. "The waiting room is full. Can I have them see Lila for now so they can—"

"Absolutely not. Reschedule everyone."

With a tiny step forward, Lila motioned to the waiting room. "I can handle it, Eric, if you'd—" She paused at the look he shot her. He waited, the stare of all stares continuing. What did he—oh, she'd called him by his first name. "I mean, Dr. Baxter. I've cared for animals by myself for the last year. Really, it's fine."

"I don't know a thing about your abilities, beyond what a piece of paper says to me. This is my livelihood. Surely you can appreciate why I would prefer to be here to ensure everything goes as planned." He continued his stare down as though he wanted her to reply to this, but Lila was rooted to the spot, so greatly offended she was tempted to tell the old man to stuff his job in that belly of his, she quit. But she needed this job, needed to be at home, and this was the only animal hospital in town.

For now.

In time, Lila hoped to open her own establishment, but that would take time. And money. Which she wasn't overrun with at the moment. So instead, she simply took a step back and smiled. "Of course. I'll just wait for you here."

"Fantastic." Then without another word, he went back to his office, grabbed a black bag, then set off out the door, Tracy well on her way to rescheduling everyone in the waiting area and Lila standing there helpless.

She'd need to gain Dr. Baxter's trust soon or she'd lose her mind out of boredom. Or go off on him. Right now, both seemed to be equal risks.

Walking into the waiting area, she paused beside Tracy and motioned to the line. "Why don't I help you get them rescheduled? Might as well do something."

They went to work rescheduling everyone in line, and then Lila helped clean up the area, wipe down the shelves, and sweep the floors. Soon it was dark out, and Tracy grabbed her purse and glanced with hesitation at Lila.

"Are you sure you don't want me to stay with you? It's your first day. I hate to leave you alone."

Lila smiled. "I'll be fine. I'll just review some things to keep me busy. No big deal. I'm sure he'll be back soon." The older woman waved good-bye and Lila went to work looking around the place, checking out what they offered, the various equipment and supplies they carried. Before long, two hours had passed with no Dr. Baxter, and Lila wasn't sure which would take her first—sleep or hunger.

For a moment, she contemplated ordering food to be delivered. Pizza. She could eat an entire pizza right now. But what if Baxter showed?

She sat down on the couch in the waiting room and took out a magazine, leaned back against the couch and sighed.

So much for her first day on the job.

Chapter Two

Charlie couldn't turn his brain off.

Ever since he'd had lunch with Lucas and his friend had told him that Lila was back in town, he found himself searching for her. Looking down the sidewalk after lunch as he walked to his truck. Watching passersby as he drove to the shop. Then, once he was parked and back inside Southern Dive, he kept finding himself by the front windows that faced the street, watching and searching and generally acting like a deranged stalker. All over a woman he hadn't seen in more than a decade.

And yet . . .

He thought of the last time he'd seen her, when he was packing up to move to the Keys, the need to leave Crestler's Key and find an adventure so great he'd felt as though he were suffocating. Added to that, Lucas had enlisted and now Charlie was stuck around town, hanging out with the girl he wasn't allowed to have and wanting to change that fact so badly he couldn't think straight.

Lila had helped him box up his things, and when it was finally time for him to hit the road, he pulled her into a hug. He couldn't help it, he needed to touch her, let her feel how much she meant to him, because he sure as hell couldn't say it. Even if Lucas was halfway across the country. It didn't matter.

So he hugged her, breathed in her sunflower and summer scent, and then when he started to release her, she gripped him tighter.

"What am I going to do without you?" she'd asked, her voice shaking, but Charlie forced himself to smile down at her, because he already knew what she would do—live. By that point, she'd been accepted to several colleges and would have the option to do whatever she wanted in life. And she should do whatever she wanted, live, dream, be. He wouldn't hold her back. So, he said good-bye to the girl in his heart and lost himself in the laid-back lifestyle of the Keys. Shorts and T-shirts and flip flops and a beer in his hand. And it was fun . . . until it wasn't anymore.

Needing something else to think about, Charlie cracked open his laptop and went to his Instagram page. The only good thing to come out of the Keys/Jade debacle was his Instagram page. Somehow that witch of a woman had helped launch him in the world of social media in a way that he never could have himself. Still, years later, after years of managing the account, he still wasn't fully comfortable putting himself out there. But it helped that he had regular followers, many of whom had travelled to Crestler's Key to shop at Southern Dive, the Littleton brothers' scuba diving equipment shop that had morphed into a clothing store for the outdoorsy type.

He surfed through his phone and pulled the photo he'd taken that morning of Henry chasing some chickens at the farm. He went through the process that felt like second nature to him now, resizing it and adding a filter and background. Then he captioned it "Tastes Like Chicken." Of course, he would have never let Henry actually get to the chickens, but the picture was hilarious all the same.

Immediately the likes and comments started coming in. There was once a time that he tried to reply to comments, keep up, but with four-hundred thousand followers and thousands of comments per photo now, he could either manage his Instagram comments or work. He couldn't do both. He chose the latter. Still, he'd keep a look out for and reply if something relevant came up. Plus, he kept a questions/comments box on Southern Dive's main website, so people could reach him if they needed to.

Once he'd sifted through the comments from yesterday's photo—he tried to post daily—he checked the stockroom to make sure no packages had come in without him knowing, then went to work making sure the store was in order, adjusting clothing racks, refolding T-shirts. By the time he was done, it was closing time.

Time to head home . . . alone. For whatever reason, that had never bothered him before, but knowing Lila was in town somewhere made him hyperaware of just how alone he was in Crestler's Key. In every way.

*   *   *

So . . . Lila was back in town. In Crestler's Key. Charlie thought of calling her, but then he had no idea if her cell had changed over the years, and he had no idea where she was staying. Had she bought a place here? Rented? Was she—

He cut himself off before his thoughts went any closer to obsessive.

Twirling his beer bottle in his hand, he stared at his wide-screen, not really watching it, and not for the first time, he wondered why he had bought it. He wasn't a TV kind of guy. He was a get-outside-and-do-something kind of guy, and nothing made him feel lazier than a damn TV. But it was nine o'clock, and the wings he'd picked up on the way home were long since gone. The truth was, he was lonely.

Lonely in a way that he hadn't felt in a long time. It was a feeling that rose up within him every time Lucas came back to town, and he felt like an idiot for missing his best friend even before he left, yet he couldn't push away the dark hole in his chest. And now he found out that not only was Lucas here for only two days, then leaving again, but his sister had returned for good, the single person who Charlie knew could fill in that hole in his heart. Not that he'd go that way with it; after all, he had once thought of her as a sister. That much hadn't been a lie. But what he didn't say to Lucas—couldn't say— was that one single night had changed that fact, and though Charlie had stopped it, he couldn't help wondering . . .

He twirled the beer in his fingers again, sure that he was just feeling shit that really meant nothing at all. Memories had a way of making you think they were real, live things, when really they were nothing more than past actions that needn't be repeated.

Especially this one.

Especially if Charlie hoped to keep his head intact.

He took another pull from his beer then grimaced, because nothing had tasted right to him since he'd seen Lucas and heard that Lila was back.

Pushing off the couch, Charlie started for the kitchen to toss the beer when his gaze fell to Henry, stretched out on the floor between the family room and kitchen in Charlie's open-floor-plan ranch house. But whereas normally Henry would be snoring, deep asleep by now, today he was groaning. Charlie bent down and scrubbed the dog's ears, but instead of edging closer to his owner, like always, the dog continued to groan, and that was when Charlie noticed the bit of foam coming out of his mouth.

It took him less than ten seconds to grab his keys, cradle his dog in his arms, and head out the door. Charlie wasn't a vet, but he'd been around animals his whole life on the farm, and he knew that whatever this was couldn't be good.

The night air was cool for spring, but Charlie hadn't thought to grab a shirt before heading out the door. No matter; it wouldn't be the first time Doc Baxter had seen him without a shirt on. Sadly. At least this time, he had on shorts instead of boxers. A shudder worked through him at the memory. And not the good kind.

Charlie had not been home a month after the Jade disaster when he'd decided the fix to the crushing weight on his chest was a distraction. Or a few distractions, as happened to be the case. And one such distraction landed him at the house of a new lady in town and absolutely no idea what the hell her name was. He'd made it through just fine, but finally she asked him to whisper her name in her ear, which should have been a red flag anyway because she kept trying to direct his game. Put a hand here, kiss me there. Then the name thing came up, and he tried to run with *sweetheart*, which resulted in a look, and his brothers had always said he had too honest a face. Well, sure enough, she tossed him out on his ass, without his clothes.

He'd left his truck in town when she insisted on driving—another red flag—and so he had no choice but to make the trek in his boxers, a full-on walk of shame in plain view of anyone in town who cared to look. And he'd almost made it home, but Doc Baxter was out late on a call to the Carlisle farm. He pulled over to offer Charlie a ride, and the rest was history.

Up until that moment with Henry in his arms, Charlie had managed to steer clear of the town's old vet beyond a few passing hellos and nods, going as far as paying his niece to take Henry to the vet so he wouldn't have to endure the look of judgment from Baxter. But desperate and all, tonight, he didn't have a choice.

Charlie unlocked his truck and opened the back seat, gingerly laying Henry down and patting his head. "You're going to be fine, boy." And then as if the universe wanted to give him the finger, the dog pulled back, his head jerking as a guttural sound rumbled from his throat, and then he puked all over the seat.

"Ah, shit." Charlie scrambled around in search of a towel, something, but coming up empty, had to run back into his house, grab some stuff to clean up, and then try to move Henry, but the poor dog groaned louder and Charlie thought *Screw it.* "The truck will live. Let's get you to Baxter."

He dropped down a few more towels onto the seat and floorboard and then jumped into the driver's seat, shifted into reverse, backing into the small turnaround to the left, then sped down his long driveway, cursing himself in that moment for wanting to live so far away from the road. And town.

In the moment, he'd wanted peace and quiet, a place where he could go to think. But now, Henry was making that guttural noise again, and Charlie feared what this might mean. Was he poisoned somehow? A virus? Could dogs catch Zika? There had been a lot of mosquitos around lately.

Taking a sharp left turn, he straightened the wheel and prepared for the long stretch of road that was Hwy 243, which led directly into Crestler's Key city limits. There wasn't a single traffic light or stop sign to deter him, until he passed the official WELCOME TO CRESTLER'S KEY sign, and then he took the next right onto Riding Lane and pulled into Baxter's office, grateful to see a light still on inside.

Charlie parked in front of the main door and jumped out. The air was heavy for spring, cloud cover mixed in with the stars in the black sky above. Another hour, and that ominous sky would be pouring down on all of Crestler's Key. As if on cue, a boom of thunder hit from miles away.

Opening the left back door of his truck, Charlie scooped up his best friend, who thankfully was still awake, giving him hope, and he pushed the door closed with his leg, then set out for the front porch. Baxter's old dog wasn't anywhere to be seen, which made Charlie wonder if he should have called before he came. Maybe the light was on, but no one was home. Why hadn't he called? Now, his cell was in the truck, so he'd have to go back, try to juggle Henry in his arms, open the truck door, get the cell, and then close it back before he could come back to this point.

Frustrated and praying God was listening, he rapped on the door several times. "Come on."

No sounds came from inside, and Henry's eyes closed in agony. Charlie's heart clenched.

He knocked again, harder this time, over and over, his head dropping. "Come on!"

"Settle down, I'm here, I'm here."

Hope burst inside Charlie at the voice, but it wasn't the cottony voice of Doc Baxter that met his ears. And it wasn't Ms. Tracy. He thought back to what Lucas had told him at lunch, about Lila joining the vet office, and as if it'd been there all along, a memory bubbled up.

They were playing in the woods behind Lucas's house and he had gotten stuck in the barbed wire fencing that surrounded one of the farms. No choice of what to do, Lucas went for help, only to return with Lila, a smirk on her face.

"You boys sure are stupid," she had said. Then when he decided he didn't need a girl to help him out. Certainly not Lucas's sister, with her brains too big for her britches and her continuous need to call out Charlie's lack of smarts. Forget that. So, he tried to yank himself free, only to get caught more, the barbed wire curling into the flesh of his arm, until he was near tears.

"Settle down, I'm here," she'd said, her touch matching her tone for the first time. He was twelve then and she was ten, but when her gaze hit his, so impossibly blue, he wasn't sure how to look away. Suddenly, he wasn't as concerned with the cuts in his arm and more with making his lungs remember how to function.

Now the animal hospital's door cracked open, and Charlie's eyes fell on the person on the other side.

"Charlie?"

For a moment, Charlie forgot why he'd come, forgot his sick dog, forgot his own freaking name. Because the Lila before him wasn't at all the thin, too tall for her age, too smart for her own good girl he remembered. Oh, no. This person, this woman, she was something else entirely. Which made him wonder if maybe this wasn't Lila at all.

His gaze fixed on her face. High cheekbones, golden-tan skin, round eyes so blue they made you lose your mind for a second. Full, pouty lips slowly spread into an easy smile, and her once-short black hair now cascaded to her waist in effortless waves that called to his fingertips to comb the strands, to pull them gently, so her chin would lift and he could see if that mouth tasted as good as it looked. Finally, he pulled his attention from her face down to the rest of her and—

"Wow."

She bit her lip in an obvious effort to keep from laughing. "Charlie . . . ?"

"Yeah?"

"The dog?"

As if he'd been shaken from a trance, Charlie startled back, narrowly dropping Henry, who groaned in his arms, and guilt punched him in the gut. "Henry's dying or something. Can you help?"

Her grin spread, so close to laughter it was embarrassing, but Charlie couldn't make his brain work properly. "Come on in. Room one, there." She backed away, holding open the door, and pointed inside to the hall and the number one sticking out from the door.

The office was quiet, no one else around. No one to see the fear Charlie felt, both over Henry and the woman before him, a woman he had once thought he would recognize anywhere, and yet there she stood, a stranger.

"Baxter, you're just going to have to get over yourself, I'm doing this," she said, and Charlie craned his neck in search of the old vet. But beyond the parrot calling away in his cage by the front desk, there was no one else in the place. No one besides him and Lila.

"Are you talking to ghosts or something? 'Cause I don't think old Baxter is here."

Lila flashed him a grin that hadn't left her face since she saw him. Her cheeks reddened. "No, sorry. I talk to myself a little." She shrugged. "Okay, a lot. Nervous habit, and you know what they say about old habits?"

Charlie set Henry on the exam table and took a step back, before running his hands through his hair. "No, can't say that I do."

Her eyes hit his, and then flipped down, holding on his bare chest. "Some old habits die hard." She cleared her throat. "So what's going on with . . . ?"

"Henry VIII, but I just call him Henry."

Pausing mid-motion, her hand still hovering over Henry, she glanced back at him. "Seriously?"

"Yes, seriously," Charlie said, pulling back with mock offense. "What's wrong with his name?"

A genuine smile crept across her face as she went back to work inspecting Henry, and Charlie tried in vain to keep from questioning everything she was doing. All he could think was that if he were puking sick, he sure wouldn't want the doctor poking him in the stomach.

"Didn't you once have a lab named Alexander the Great?" She continued her inspection, and when Henry groaned, Charlie placed his hands on his head, his stomach muscles tightening.

"Yes. When did you say Baxter was getting here?"

"A history of choosing bad pet names. Interesting." She peeked at him again, waiting for him to defend his choice of names, but what could he say? Who the hell wanted a dog around named Fido or Sam? No one with imagination, that was for sure. "I didn't say when Baxter would be here, mainly because I don't have the faintest clue. He's at Carlisle Farms."

Damn Carlisles.

"Right. But you're trained and stuff? Lucas said you finished vet school, so you're good to do this, right?" Charlie cringed as she pulled out several metal things that looked a lot like torture instruments and went to work checking Henry's eyes and ears and generally making the poor dog all the more miserable.

She smiled. "So let me get this straight, only a man can be a veterinarian in your eyes? Not a woman? Or if a woman is, she couldn't possibly be as trained as the man."

"Wait, wait, wait. I didn't say—"

"Sure you didn't. You just thought it." She set down one of her torture devices with a slight bang, but when she turned on him, she was still grinning. "As chauvinistic as ever. Just like that name you used to call me. Tiny. Again, what kind of name is that?"

Charlie bit back a grin at the memory of the name and the first time he'd used it. They were outside on the old tire swing and were talking about climbing the big oak it hung from. She had wanted to join Charlie and Lucas, but Charlie had told her she was too tiny to climb the tree. She punched him in the stomach and asked how tiny she looked now, causing her brother to break out in fits of laughter. The name stuck. "Hey, I'm not—"

She tossed up a hand. "Save it. But your sweet dog here is going to be fine. I'm guessing he ate something he shouldn't have. Maybe in the yard? He should be all better in twenty-four hours, but if not, bring him back in to see me."

"You mean to see me."

Their eyes fell on Baxter, as grumpy as ever, and standing in the doorway with a glare at Lila that made Charlie step between them on instinct to protect her. Sighing loudly, she huffed and walked around him.

"I can take care of myself," she murmured.

"What exactly do you think you're doing?" Baxter screamed. "Trying to get me sued!"

Lila flinched, and Charlie's face split with a grin. "Sure you can." Then he went over and scooped Henry back up, and started for the door. "Seeing as how Henry here will be fine, I'll just let you two get back to . . . whatever this is. Baxter," he said, nodding to the vet. Then his eyes shifted over to Lila. "Tiny."

She crossed her arms, her eyes narrowing, and he couldn't keep the laugh from escaping him or the smile from lingering on his lips long after he'd pulled away.

Chapter Three

After an epic browbeating by Dr. Baxter, and an impressive showing of calm, cool, and collected by Lila, she headed home. Though her "home" was less a home and more a rented apartment over Annie-Jean Carlisle's garage. The older woman liked to stop by unannounced, but since she was part owner of AJ&P Bakery, she always brought over pies or cookies or freshly baked breads for Lila to try. Then she'd grill Lila about her life.

She suspected Annie-Jean, who had always been spunky, was not so much nosy as she was lonely. It made Lila wish she could find Annie-Jean a man. In fact, she was adding that to her list.

At the next stop sign Lila paused, because it wasn't like anyone was coming from one of the other directions anyway, and pulled her planner from her bag. She flipped to her CK goals page and read through the list.

1. Beg Dr. Baxter to hire her.
   Success! Or . . . kind of. Of course, he still insisted that she was going to get him sued and that she couldn't actually touch an animal. But in time, she'd impress him with her charm. Or if that didn't work, she'd call Mrs. Baxter.
2. Find a place to live.
   Sort of a success. Annie had agreed to let her live there as long as she needed, but Lila hoped to be in her own place within the next six months. She wasn't vying for love anytime soon, maybe ever, but she sure couldn't imagine bringing a man back to Annie's house, when Annie might pop in without warning.
3. Scout out a place to open her own business.
   She needed a solid year in at Baxter's to really learn what Crest-

ler's Key's business traffic was like, but in that year she intended to explore all her options, get her financing in order,
and then she'd let Baxter know she was quitting. Of course that
was assuming he didn't fire her first. And that she acquired
some regular clientele. See item 1 about charming Baxter.

4. Go to the shooting range and buy a gun. Or maybe a Taser. Or
   maybe just a can of pepper spray.

   Lucas had been on her ever since the incident in Charlotte that
   she needed to protect herself, that he wasn't around all the time,
   and he'd feel better if she was carrying. The problem wasn't
   that Lila didn't know her way around a gun—her daddy and
   Lucas had insisted she learn how to shoot. But she wasn't as
   well-trained or comfortable with them as Lucas. Plus, he just
   liked guns. They were interesting to him, fascinating, like a
   hobby. To Lila, they were a mistake waiting to happen, and
   she refused to carry one or even own one until that fear had
   been overcome. Which, let's be honest, might never happen.
   She wasn't anti-gun. She was anti-Lila-with-a-gun.

5. Call Charlie Littleton.

   She wasn't sure why Charlie had found his way onto her list,
   but she knew that she wanted to see him. She wanted to see if
   he was still the free-spirited boy she remembered. Though he
   owned the farm with his brothers, she suspected that wasn't
   his thing, and she was eager to learn what he was up to now.
   Even if he were Lucas's best friend, and Lucas would freak
   out if he knew she was having any thoughts at all about Charlie. Of course, the calling hadn't happened—yet.

But she *had* seen him.

Her thoughts drifted back to the hospital and seeing him outside
on the porch, wearing nothing but a pair of gym shorts and worry on
his face. Her attention went immediately to the dog, and for a beat
she didn't realize that he wasn't wearing a shirt. But then he set
Henry on the exam table and stepped back, revealing an impeccably
built body, and suddenly Lila forgot how to breathe. Her eyes
scanned down his bare chest, hills and valleys and contours in all the
right places, and her brain refused to work. She was transported to
that fateful day when she'd almost kissed him, that crush of hers taking over, and for a second, she thought he wanted to kiss her back,

she could see it on his face, and her pitiful heart surged. But then he looked away, his head down, his eyes closed tightly before returning to hers, and she could see the rejection on his face long before he opened his mouth.

Shuddering, she forced her thoughts away from Charlie and his name and down to the number six, which had been empty. Quickly she wrote out her sixth goal and task.

6. Find Ms. Annie a man.

She was reaching over to put the planner back in her bag when a horn sounded from behind her and she jumped, her eyes darting to the rearview mirror, another memory bubbling up before she could push it back. Darkness. Someone approaching. Fear so real it sucked the oxygen from her lungs.

Her hands clenched around the steering wheel as the horn honked again, and then the door of the car behind her opened, and Lila started to take off, before she caught the person waving her arms frantically, and Lila's fear-stricken face quickly switched to a smile. She pushed her own door open and stepped out, taking off, until she reached the woman and then they were talking all at once.

"When did you get here?"

"How did you know it was me?"

"I can't believe you're finally back!"

"I can't believe it's you!"

Hugging the woman tightly once more, Lila stepped back and peered down at her tiny best friend, Audrey, the spitting image of the famous Audrey Hepburn even all these years later.

"You scared the crap out of me."

Audrey's brown eyes narrowed as she pulled back.

"Lord, why would you be scared here? Did you forget where you are? This isn't that big city life you had in Charlotte."

Big city life in Charlotte? Most people wouldn't consider Charlotte an especially big city. Midsized, maybe, but nowhere near the population of Atlanta or Boston or New York. Which was maybe why Lila never worried over her safety there, but she learned the hard way that insanity can live and breathe anywhere. In Crestler's Key, though? Maybe not. She hoped not, but all the same she would be on her guard. Always.

Lila released her friend and ran a hand over her face. Audrey grabbed the hand and held it out, staring as it continued to tremble despite Lila's strict instruction to stop.

"You're shaking."

The sky had long since turned dark, with gray storm clouds hovering overhead, the look ominous and threatening. Besides the occasional car passing in the distance, there were no other sounds around them. Perhaps, the occasional cricket or wind through the trees, but otherwise it was quiet, peaceful. Nothing about Crestler's Key suggested danger, and Lila knew that, yet she couldn't get her heart to slow down. In truth, it hadn't slowed down in more than six months, and that single problem was one of the reasons she'd moved back to Crestler's Key in the first place. She needed to find comfort, to remember how to breathe again, to close her eyes without fearing what she'd find when she reopened them. And only one place brought that kind of relief. Or more specifically, only one person.

Charlie.

Lucas also made her feel safe, but once he joined the army and moved up to the Special Forces divisions, she found herself more afraid *for* him than comforted *by* him. Which left only Charlie, the boy who'd always been around, always looking after her, always able to slow down her racing heart and remind her that fear lived in your chest, not in the world. Only that wasn't really true, something Lila would never forget.

"Lila."

Snapping herself out of the daze, she waved her hand through the air and tried to laugh, playing off the reaction as nothing. "Stupid nightmare last night still has me freaked out."

She could tell her friend wasn't convinced, but Audrey had always been the kind of person to listen, never push. "All right. Well, I was heading over to Maguire's to meet up with the girls. Want to come?"

"The girls?"

Lila tried to ignore the sting of jealousy in her chest that her best friend now had new girls to call best friends. It wasn't Audrey's fault that Lila left for college, then vet school, then work. What did she expect, her friend to never befriend another person? No, she would never want that, but still . . .

"Yeah, Harper and Sophie are new to town since you were here, but you know Ella. Kate and Emery were supposed to join us, but something came up with their kids."

Lila nodded. She hadn't seen Kate Littleton in a long time, but she was always very sweet. A teacher now, Lila thought, and there couldn't be a better profession for her. Zac, the eldest brother, was always domineering, forever a leader. He ran the farm. And then Brady, the youngest, always pretended to be wild, but really he was a lot like Charlie. Charlie wasn't wild in the least, but he was a true free spirit, a creature of nature. Both he and Brady could have been happy on some beach somewhere, a drink in their hands as they stared at the water, waiting for their next adventure.

Lila wasn't sure if any of the Littleton brothers had married, though she knew Kate had married a Hamilton from Triple Run. And then at the animal hospital, Lila didn't notice a ring on Charlie's finger, which gave her more joy than it should.

"So you'll come? Please come."

Glancing back at her car, then up at the night sky, Lila contemplated what she wanted to do. In truth, she wanted to go back to her apartment at Annie's, change into PJ's, and get lost in an episode of *Gilmore Girls*. Nothing about her life was flashy now, and though she knew her idea of "fun" would be classified as old and boring to anyone else her age, she liked to make it inside, check the closets and under the bed, lock the doors. It gave her comfort, something in short supply these days. "It might rain," she said finally, knowing it was a thin excuse.

"Not inside the bar," Audrey said with a smirk.

Lila's lips twitched. "You always were such a smartass."

"You love me."

"I do. And I've missed you."

Audrey reached out and grasped her hand. "Me, too, love. Please come hang out. I want to catch up. Lots to discuss since you left. Just a drink or two and they have fantastic wings. It'll be fun."

Fun sounded like something in a book or movie at this point, nothing that could be real in Lila's world, but what the heck. The only person she'd hung out with since she arrived in Crestler's Key was Annie, and though she adored the woman and her cooking, Lila could use some true girl time. Besides, eventually, she would have to push herself outside of her comfort zone; otherwise, she might never recover enough to become her old self again.

"Okay, I'm in."

They decided for both women to drive, so Lila could leave if she wanted, which—let's face it—was a very strong possibility. She needed to get out, but she also liked to be alone. Well, alone until Annie chose to use her spare key and make herself at home in the apartment, whether Lila was up for a visit or not.

Parking around back of Maguire's beside Audrey's red convertible, Lila stepped out, locked her car, and then came to a halt. Her eyes traveled down, from her too-dressy blouse, to her too-professional skirt. She was not at all dressed in bar-appropriate clothes. Or even dinner-appropriate clothes.

"Um, I'm a mess." She motioned to her clothes and then Audrey, who was perfectly trendy in an easy skirt and tank top, sandals completing the look. No one in Crestler's Key would dress skimpy, even at a bar, but still, there was an expected easiness that went with a bar look—fitted jeans, heels, cute top. Skirt, tank, sandals, like Audrey. Something.

But Lila was still dressed in her work attire—dress skirt and blouse, heels. *Boring.*

Audrey scanned her up and down, cocked her head in thought, then snapped her fingers. "Okay, we can work with this. Totally work with it. Do you have a tank under that shirt?" she asked and Lila couldn't help but grin that her friend still knew her so well.

"Always."

Audrey beamed. "I knew it. Okay, good, shed the outer layer."

Lila unbuttoned her work blouse to reveal a black tank top, and then she remembered with a touch of horror that below the black tank, she'd worn a new black lace bralette. She'd bought one from Victoria's Secret after the second time Annie had popped in unannounced—this time with Marty, the mailman—and found Lila in her PJ shorts and white tank top without a bra.

Double embarrassment.

She vowed then to wear a bra at all times, but no woman could comfortably wear a devil-bra all the time, so she bought the bralette. Only when she received it, it was so comfy that it spoiled her. She quickly ordered four more and hadn't worn a devil-bra since.

Now Audrey's eyes bulged, a slow smile spreading. "What is that adorableness? Turn around."

Lila did as instructed and remembered the high-neck back with intricate lace detailing.

"That is so pretty! Where did you get it? I need one."

Lila grinned. "Victoria's Secret, but I'll warn you, you'll never wear a normal bra again. They're addictive."

"Yeah, that settles it. I'm ordering one tonight." She eyed Lila's outfit again, then went back to her car, popped the trunk, and pulled out a pair of sparkly black sandals. "Same size as me, right?"

God love her. What had Lila done without Audrey for the last several years? Clearly, her fashion sense had suffered, but what else? It had been a long time since she'd hung out with girls and talked about girlie things.

Slipping on the pretty sandals, she stared down at her new outfit—black skirt, black tank, and black sandals. Not half bad. It worked with her tan, and at least she didn't have her work outfit on anymore. Mostly.

They walked around to the front of the bar, taking the sidewalk, and with each step Lila felt her pulse speeding up, her nerves twisting. It had been a long time since she'd been here. What would the town think of her now?

Music poured out from the bar as they reached the front door, already open from someone else slipping inside before them. Thankfully, Charlie wouldn't be here, so at least she wouldn't have to be on her A game. If she even had an A game, anymore.

Audrey waved to a group of women around a raised-top table close to the bar, and they started over, Lila's nerves twisting again as she peered around.

This is Crestler's Key, she told herself. Safer than safe. Plus, her brother was in town, and he could drop a person by look alone. Everything was okay.

"Lila!" Ella stood and started for her, and Lila grinned as she hugged her old friend. "We're so excited you're back. Are you here for good? I heard Old Baxter is giving you grief."

Wow, talk travelled fast. She'd forgotten how quickly gossip spread here. Back in Charlotte, no one knew anyone else's business. It was nice, and she'd enjoyed her time there, until . . . *I'm not going to think about it. Not now.*

Lila shrugged. "I'm working him down. But yes, back for good."

"This is Harper," Ella said, motioning to the red-headed woman beside her, her look natural and very Crestler's Key. Lila imagined she fit in perfectly the moment she stepped foot inside town limits. "And this is Sophie."

Lila's gaze cut over to the woman beside Harper, her ultra-blond hair flowing down her back in waves, her face perfectly made up, a wicked glint in her eyes that Lila suspected never went away. It must have been an experience to watch the town's reaction to her.

"Hey, you," Sophie said, like they were old friends. "I was wondering when I'd get to meet the famous Lila Jacobs."

"Famous?" Lila's eyes widened.

Sophie's ruby-red lips spread into a smile. "Yeah, Charlie talks about you and Lucas all the time."

Her heart clenched. "You know Charlie?" Sophie didn't look like Charlie's type but then Lila didn't really know Charlie anymore, now did she? His type could have changed. He could have changed.

But then before she could dwell on it more, Audrey piped up. "Sophie's engaged to Zac Littleton," she said, likely sensing Lila's unease. Though they rarely talked about it, Audrey knew Lila had crushed on Charlie all her childhood and teen years.

"Wow, that's amazing. Zac is a great guy," Lila said, unable to hide her relief, and a knowing look crossed Sophie's face.

"This is going to be fun," she said, and Lila looked around as though she'd missed something.

"What's going to be fun?" Maybe she meant the wedding planning, that sort of thing.

A look of absolute glee took over Sophie's face, like she'd just found herself in the middle of a challenge she couldn't refuse. "Oh, nothing." Then she nodded to the bar. "I'll get you a drink. What are you having?"

"She'll have a Corona with lime. Same as me," Audrey said, then she paused and looked over at Lila. "Or I guess that could have changed. There's so much I don't know about you now." Her mouth turned down in a frown, but Lila quickly spoke up.

"Sadly, I haven't changed all that much. Terrible, isn't it? But yeah, a Corona would be great."

Sophie beamed. Clearly her resting face was a smile. "Two Coronas coming up. Anyone else need anything?" She eyed the table, but Harper was still nursing a fruity drink with an umbrella and Ella shook her head.

"I'm good. I think Maguire put double the alcohol in this thing," Ella said, shaking her cocktail. "It'll be a miracle if I don't have a hangover tomorrow, and this is my first drink."

They all laughed, and then Sophie bopped over to the bar, her move almost giddy.

"What's she so excited about?" Lila asked, glancing over at Sophie with intrigue.

"She's like a town matchmaker on steroids," Audrey said. "It's like she's happy now so she wants everyone else to be, too."

"Aw, that's kind of nice," Lila said. "Who's she trying to fix up?" She was still watching Sophie, so she didn't notice that all three women were staring her down until she peered over at Audrey, then did a double take at the grin on her face.

"No. Not me. I just got here. Who would she want to set me up with?"

Audrey laughed. "You're kidding, right? You're back in town, the only girl Charlie Littleton has ever talked about with any real interest, and our fine matchmaker, Sophie, is marrying his brother. It's like kismet."

"What?" Thank God Lila didn't have her drink yet, or she would have spit it everywhere. "Me and Charlie? No, no, no. That's crazy." Jerking back, Lila stared around the bar, hopeful no one had heard what she'd said. Especially someone by the name of Charlie. Or a friend of Charlie's. Or anyone who might at all know Charlie. Which, crap, described everyone in the town.

Her cheeks burned and she tried to clear her face of any unwanted emotions that might reveal how very much Lila would have loved the idea of being with Charlie . . . six months ago. Now she wasn't—couldn't—well, she didn't really know what she was anymore, but dateable certainly wasn't on the table. Not now, maybe not ever if she couldn't shake the panic in her chest every time she thought about it.

"The way I see it, it's crazy y'all haven't gotten together yet," Sophie said as she set down the two beers and took her own seat, some pink concoction in her hand that Lila suspected Maguire had never made prior to Sophie requesting it. She read as the kind of woman who knew who she was and wasn't about to stand down on her wants for anyone. Zac was in trouble.

"No, seriously. It really isn't like that." Lila took a long pull of her beer, then two, because clearly she needed alcohol in her veins to survive this conversation.

"But you like him, right? Or is that in the past?"

She choked on her beer, sputtering as she glared over at her old best friend. The key word there *old*, because Lila might not talk to Audrey again after this outing. Clearly, Harper, Ella, and Sophie were trustworthy people for Audrey, but Lila didn't know them. Not really, and certainly not enough to talk about Charlie.

"It's been a long time since I thought about Charlie like that."

Lie.

"Honestly, I didn't think he still lived here."

Lie.

"Charlie's the furthest thing from my mind."

I am so going to hell.

Sophie's eyes flashed with excitement, like Lila had said exactly what she wanted to hear. Clearly, she'd need to work on her poker face around these ladies if she hoped to hide her true feelings. "Well, you might not have thought about him, but he's definitely thought about you. Probably thinking about you right now, by the way he's looking around this bar."

This bar? Did she just say *this* bar?

Lila spun around so fast she almost fell out of her chair, but not before Sophie threw her hand into the air and called out, "Charlie!"

And suddenly his eyes snapped to the table, scanning, until they landed on Lila, and then he was coming toward them.

Chapter Four

Charlie's eyes fell on Lila, the bit of black lace peeking out from her tank top, her hair tousled and loose around her shoulders, those bright blue eyes staring back at him, and suddenly he wasn't sure why he'd come there. Hell, he could scarcely remember to breathe.

He cleared his throat in hopes that it would settle him down, but as he started toward her, his heartbeat kicked up instead, until he stood over her, her perfect chin tilted up to look at him, her plump lips curved into a smile that lit her entire face. And damn. What was he thinking again?

"Hey there, little brother."

His attention flicked over to Sophie, who still drove him insane despite Zac's insistence that she wasn't so bad. "Not yet. And even then, no."

"You love me, admit it. I'm the sister you never had."

"I have a sister."

"Oh. Right." She giggled, and he thought he ought to call Zac now to prepare him for the drunk call he'd likely receive in an hour, when the buzz she was showing now turned downright messy. Sophie was all spark and fire, and though Charlie had grown to appreciate what his brother saw in her, she would never have been his type.

Unlike the dark-haired woman sitting in front of him.

Lila was sassy, too, but in a more understated way. In fact, everything about her was understated. She was beautiful in a way that spoke for itself. She didn't need loads of makeup or styled hair to show the world that she was gorgeous. That smile of hers told the story all on its own.

And now he was staring again. Damn it all to hell, he needed a drink to settle his nerves before he did something stupid. Like make a move on his best friend's little sister. As though the thought of Lucas had been the cold shower he needed, he remembered why he'd come to Maguire's in the first place.

"So what's up with you, then? Looking for someone?" Sophie waggled her eyebrows and then glanced at Lila and grinned again.

Clearly, he would need to ask Zac to get his fiancée under control before Lila figured out that Charlie talked about her a little more than he should. Or a lot more than he should. Ignoring Sophie, he focused back on Lila and forced his brain to work instead of absorbing another detail about her. Like the cute-as-heck freckle beside her right eye. Damn, he was in so much trouble, and she just returned to town. "Actually, Lucas sent me looking for you. Said he called you a few times."

She pulled back. "Oh. I must have turned my phone off." Fumbling through her bag, she pulled out her phone, turned it back on, and then her eyebrows knitted together in obvious concern.

"He called five times. Did something happen?" She bit her lip and peered back up at him, but Charlie was too lost in her mouth and those white teeth clamped down over her naturally rosy lips to hear her.

"Sorry, what?"

It was Sophie who answered, getting far too much joy out of this exchange. "She asked if something happened. You all right there, Charlie? You seem a little . . . distracted." She laughed again, and he glared back at her, praying she could read minds along with that superpower of hers to wreck his mood. But instead of saying anything to his soon-to-be sister-in-law, he focused back on Lila.

"I don't know. He just called me and asked if I'd seen you, then said he needed to talk to you. Both of us, actually. And so I said I'd find you and we'd head to his house."

Immediately, she stood, grabbed her bag, and faced the girls. "Sorry to cut this short, but this doesn't sound like Lucas. Okay if I head out to find out what's going on?"

"Of course," Audrey said. "Call and let me know, okay?"

"I will." They hugged and then Charlie and Lila headed back out.

Charlie followed Lila outside, then down the sidewalk toward his truck. "That one's me," he said, motioning to it.

"He's been deployed again, hasn't he?"

Worry seeped through Charlie's mind, coursing through him, until it settled in his stomach like a virus that would have him up all night. "Honestly? I don't know. He didn't say."

She nodded and slipped into the passenger seat, her spine pencil straight, her eyes trained out the windshield. "I can feel it, ya know? Five deployments in three years, and it never gets easier to hear him say good-bye."

The pain in her voice made Charlie wish they were closer, that he could pull her to him and help her work through this before she saw her brother. Because he knew firsthand how hard it was to say good-bye to Lucas, never knowing the specifics of where he was going or how long he would be gone. Never knowing if he would make it back home.

But Charlie also knew that Lucas loved his sister more than anything, and it would destroy him to see her breakdown over him leaving. He'd worry, and wherever Lucas was going, he didn't need to worry about home.

"I'm not going to cry."

Charlie glanced over and then back to the road. "It's all right if you need to, though. I get it."

She shook her head, cleared her throat, and tucked her chin for a moment before focusing out the windshield again. "No. If he can be strong enough to go protect our country on whatever insanely dangerous mission they've assigned to him, then I can be strong enough to put on a tough-girl face and say good-bye to him without falling apart. It's the least I can do for him. I wouldn't want him to worry about me and then he—he—" She drew a sharp breath and clenched her fists.

"Hey." Without thinking, Charlie reached over and took her hand in his, squeezing tightly. "We don't even know what this is yet. Don't let yourself get upset. At least not yet."

She turned toward him for the first time. "Lucas called me five times. Then called you to come find me. At ten o'clock at night."

All right, she had him there. "It could be—"

"He's getting deployed, Charlie. You know it as well as I do."

They fell into silence as Charlie pulled down Lucas's gravel driveway, every light in the house on, which was another bad sign.

Lucas was a power hoarder. He hated to waste anything, so if he was this awake and active this late at night, then it must mean he was packing.

Charlie was still holding Lila's hand when they parked, but he released it as soon as Lucas stepped outside, a tinge of guilt working through his stomach. But he reminded himself that he was just comforting her, not making a move on her. Even if he'd felt like doing just that only minutes before at the bar. Damn, he needed to get his head on straight. They'd seen each other twice since she had gotten back, but those two occurrences had hit him like a freight train, all those old, pent-up feelings toward her resurfacing.

Stepping out, Charlie tucked his hands into his jeans pockets, an old Rolling Stones T-shirt and flip flops completing his look, because while he wasn't at the beach anymore, he'd never stop dressing the part.

"Thank God," Lucas said, starting toward them. He pulled Lila into a big hug. "Didn't think I'd get to see you before I left." He checked his watch, cringed, and then glanced back at his sister.

"I knew it," she said. "When do you leave?"

Lucas took a step back and ran a hand over his buzzed head. "Ten minutes."

She nodded, though Charlie could tell she was holding in her emotions. "Any clues how long you'll be gone or where you're going?"

The storm that had been threatening earlier boomed overhead again, tiny droplets of rain beginning to fall. The air smelled like earth and air and peacefulness, and yet as Charlie's gaze landed on Lila and held, he didn't feel peaceful. He felt pain.

Cocking his head, Lucas reached out for her hand. "You know I can't say."

She nodded again, but this time her bottom lip began to tremble.

"Ah, Tiny, don't cry. Please. You know I'm the toughest bastard out there. Ain't nobody gonna hurt me."

Charlie cleared his throat. "Dude, you are not even close to the toughest bastard out there. That role's been filled since we were six years old and your pansy ass refused to go into Old Richardson's haunted house."

Lucas eyed him, a crooked grin easing the tension in his face. "I'm the pansy ass, huh? Clearly you don't remember peeing your pants on the Spidartron at Six-Flags in fifth grade."

Lila laughed as she eyed Charlie. "He's got you there. I'll never forget us having to hit the water ride to hide your wet stain." She laughed still louder, and Charlie and Lucas exchanged a knowing look, their plan to distract her working. They were always a good team when it came to Lila. Together teaching her to ride a bike. Together threatening boys who broke her heart. Together moving her into her college dorm.

"Care if I talk to this asshole alone for a sec?" Lucas said to Lila.

She glanced between them. "Um, sure. Plotting your world domination?"

Charlie winked. "You know it."

Lila started on inside, and Lucas waited until the screen door closed behind her to turn on his best friend. His face was serious, more serious than normal.

"Look, I need a favor."

"Anything," Charlie said without hesitation.

"Need you to take care of Lila."

Charlie's eyes went wide and a smirk broke across his face. "What kind of care are we talking about here?"

Lucas punched him in the chest, jokingly but the dude was a Green Beret, so Charlie felt that shit deep. "Damn perv. She's my sister."

"Just making sure we were talking about the same thing is all." He flashed Lucas a grin.

"Nah, seriously though," Lucas said. "She's been through a lot. Not really wanting me to talk about it, so I won't. But I'd feel better if I knew someone was here looking out for her. Can I count on you?"

Charlie grinned again, and Lucas pointed at him. "Not like that. In fact, add that to the list—look after her and keep your hands to yourself. The last thing I need is to come back to a sister with a broken heart because my best friend couldn't keep his dick in his pants."

"Hey, I take offense." Charlie crossed his arms to further his point, though he couldn't stop the nagging voice in his head that said Lucas was onto something here and likely had a right to put his friend in place.

"Just look after her for me. She's in a vulnerable state right now. I need to know she's okay."

Charlie patted Lucas's shoulder. "All joking aside, you know I'm here for her. I'd never let anything happen to her. You know that."

Lucas nodded. "I know. Which is why I pushed for her to move here. At least if I can't be around her, you would be. I trust you more than anyone. More than a brother."

And just like that, Charlie knew he had no choice but to tuck the idea of Lila away. He wouldn't risk breaking his best friend's trust.

"I've got your back."

Lucas eyed his watch again, and then back at the house. "Damn, I gotta go."

"We need you to be careful, okay? I know you will be. But Lila's not the only one who worries about your sorry self."

They hugged as Lila stepped back outside. "Am I allowed out here again or am I breaking up the bro-fest?"

"Damn, this is going to be painful. She's as much a smartass as you."

"Worse," Lucas said with a grin, and then Lila pushed him, before pulling him into a hug.

"Be careful."

Lucas placed his bag into his Jeep, and then hugged each of them again.

"Love you, little sister."

"Love you, big brother."

He and Charlie clasped hands and then hugged. "Be back when I can. You'll lock up for me?" he asked Lila, who nodded yes. They waved as he got into his truck and shut the door, and then he drove away. Every time this happened, Charlie wondered if it would be the last time he would see him, and every time he'd curse himself for thinking it. Today was no different.

"He asked you to look after me, didn't he?" She wiped away a stray tear, then another.

"Yeah, but I told him he should be asking you to look after me. You, Tiny Girl, can take care of yourself." She laughed, but it soon turned into a sob, and Charlie pulled her to him, holding her close to his chest.

"What if he doesn't—?"

"*Shh.*" Charlie ran his hands over her hair and held her tighter. "Don't even think it. He's coming home. And we'll be here, ready to celebrate with him when he gets here."

She pulled away. "You really think so?"

Charlie swiped his thumb under each of her eyes to wipe away her tears. "I know it. No one's tougher than Lucas. Couldn't tell him that, ego and all. But I would bet my life on it. He's coming home."

She nuzzled into his chest again, and Charlie placed his chin on top of her head. He would keep his word to protect Lila, at all costs. Now if he could keep his other agreement and keep his hands and feelings to himself.

Lila drew a breath, allowing Charlie's all-man, slightly lemony, 100 percent sexy scent flood her senses until, little by little, she felt better. She inhaled again, eager for more, when Charlie cleared his throat and she glanced up at him to find a crooked grin staring back at her.

"Are you smelling me?" he asked, his tone light.

She recoiled. "No."

"Kind of looked like you were. The question is whether you were smelling me in a good way or a bad way, but it looked like you were a second away from licking me, which hints at good."

Lila pushed him back and shook her head. "Always Mr. Arrogant."

"Always Ms. Denial."

They squared off, but both were smiling, and she shook her head again. "You were always good at that, weren't you?"

"What?"

This time when she glanced back up at him, it was with tenderness in her eyes. "Making me feel better. No matter what it was, you could say something, distract me, and suddenly I forgot why I was upset in the first place."

Charlie took a step toward her. "Remember that time you tried out for cheerleading? But you were the most uncoordinated person imaginable?" Then he put his hands in the air and started screaming, "Gooo Tigers! T-I-G-E-R-S Tigers!" Lila swiped at him, but he ducked out of reach, laughing. "And then you twisted your ankle trying to do one of those cart-around things."

"They're called cartwheels, jerk."

"And you called me to come get you, because Lucas was retaking a test, and couldn't take you to the hospital, because you said you'd broken it. I carried you to my truck and took you home and iced you back to health. Come to think of it, I'm the one that should have been the doctor."

Lila rolled her eyes. "You just wanted to stroke my leg and cop a feel. I know your kind."

He tucked her hair behind her ear. "Oh, yeah, and what kind is that?" He glanced down at her, and then all of a sudden he straightened and took a giant step back, his eyes anywhere but on her. "Anyway, ready to get back?"

What just happened?

Lila tried to get his attention, but she could tell that he'd checked out, disappeared back inside that head of his. Which was always one of her problems—she wanted him, but he never let her in, never even considered her as a possibility. "Actually, can you just take me to my car? I don't really feel like hanging out anymore."

He finally met her questioning gaze. "Are you all right? Because I can stay with you if you need? You know, on the couch or whatever." He blew out a breath and ran a hand through his hair. If Lila didn't know any better, she'd guess he was nervous. But that was stupid.

"That's okay. I'm turning in early. Plus, Annie is there. Did you know I was living at Annie's? Over the detached garage, and she likes to walk in on me in the most inopportune times imaginable. Which could be awkward if we . . ." *What did I just say!* "And did you know she sleeps with her .22? She told me when I moved in never to walk into the main house unannounced or I'd risk getting shot!" And now she was rambling—awesome.

But the idea of Charlie at her place—well, Annie's place, but her for-now place—and him acting all nervous about it made her heart perk up and that annoying voice in the back of her head ask the question: *Maybe?*

Charlie was staring at her now, a full-on, mega-watt smile spread across his face. "First off, yes, I knew Annie slept with her .22. Got the thing when a raccoon snuck into her garage—the attached one, not the detached you're living over. But no, I didn't know you were living there. And secondly—" The grin slanted, his eyes flashing with flirtation. "What exactly did you think we'd be doing that would make it awkward if Annie walked in?" His eyebrows lifted as he waited for the answer, and Lila contemplated crawling into the ditch by the road and hiding until Charlie left. But clearly he was enjoying this too much to let it go. "Is my tiny girl having less than tiny thoughts?"

Lila shook her head and started for the truck, then remembered she had to lock up Lucas's place and shut out the lights, pivoted and marched to the front porch. "What does that even mean? And no, Mr. Arrogant. Not every thought every woman has is about you. Certainly not mine." Good God, she needed to avoid Charlie before her nose started growing from all these lies.

He was right behind her, his warmth radiating against her back as he reached around her for the door to open it. "I'm not saying all women. All right, maybe all women. But I'm specifically talking about you." And then they stepped inside, and it was like someone flipped a switch in Charlie, and his cocky smile turned to a frown.

"What are you . . . ?" Lila followed his stare to the shelves framing the widescreen across from them, and a photo of the two of them—Charlie and Lucas—in high school, arms draped over each other's shoulders, more brothers than friends, sat dead center on the right-hand shelf. "You okay?"

"What? Oh—yeah. Fine." He shook his head and once again ran his hands through his hair, an obvious nervous tic, and Lila found herself wondering what was going through his mind. "Look, just remembered that I have some place to be."

"At ten thirty? On a school night?" she teased, but when Charlie didn't return her laugh, she knew something had gotten to him. Maybe he was as worried about Lucas as she was and being here, in Lucas's house, made it worse. She didn't know. "I'll just lock up if you want to wait in the truck."

"Why don't I go turn the water off?" he asked.

"All right." She turned around so she wouldn't have to see the awkward expression on Charlie's face anymore. Already she felt uneasy around him, but now he was darting from the carefree, flirty Charlie she knew to the uncomfortable, awkward man she'd just witnessed too quickly for her to keep up. Writing it off, Lila went to work shutting off the lights, checking that the air conditioner was on, but set to eighty, and then locking the front door.

The night air had turned chilly, and the rain that had teased them earlier was coming down now in sheets. Lila took off running for the truck and slipped inside, her clothes wet and her hair hanging around her face in shiny tendrils.

"Wow, cold." She grinned as she peered over at Charlie, but he was staring down, refusing to look at her. He shook his head, muttered something, and then put the truck in drive.

Chapter Five

L ila woke at six the next morning, the remnants of a dream still circling around her. Charlie, a look, everything freezing around them. Never had Lila considered that she would still have such strong feelings for him, but the moment she saw him it was like they all came rushing back, and so far, being around him had only amplified her opinion of him.

Young Charlie was daring, funny, always there for those he cared about, but adult Charlie? He was something else entirely. First, his care for his dog; then coming to Maguire's to get her; then holding her while she cried after Lucas left. It was as though he'd changed in the best possible ways. Everything about him from before was still there, just below the surface, but as a man, he was—

She had just walked out of her bedroom to grab coffee before work, when she stopped short in the opening to the hallway, her eyes wide.

"Um, Annie?"

Annie lowered her newspaper and peered at Lila. "Honey, I thought you'd never wake up. I brought you some muffins." She pushed a plate down the kitchen counter without looking, and Lila jumped to grab it before it crashed to the ground. "And your mama called from Florida. I told her you were fine, that you'd call her later."

"Thank you?" Lila glanced around the kitchen, then the family room. It wasn't big by any scope of the imagination, but being able to see everything was one of the reasons Lila chose it. A family room, a kitchen, a bedroom, and a bathroom. That was it. Which meant there weren't very many places to hide.

Since her parents now lived in Florida, they wanted her to move in with Lucas, but Lila insisted that she needed her own place—or some semblance of her own place.

"Marty isn't here with you again, is he?"

Annie's brow furrowed. "Like I'd talk to that man again after what he did."

Uh-oh. "What did he do?" Lila turned on her Keurig and faced Annie as it heated up.

"I don't want to talk about it. And I don't know why you bother with those things. You know French press coffeemakers produce the best coffee."

Um, yeah, if you like your coffee on the ridiculous side of strong. But Lila knew better than to argue with Annie over anything related to anything inside the kitchen. Instead, she attempted to change the subject. "How are things at the bakery? I hear you're—"

Annie slammed down her paper and crossed her arms, and Lila's eyebrows went to her hairline. She wondered if something bad had happened at AJ&P or between her and Patty. It wouldn't be the first time. Years ago, Annie and Patty were best friends and had a falling out. Annie stopped speaking to Patty, and Patty moved to Triple Run and opened her own bakery there. Well, with the rivalry between the two towns that was like slapping Annie in the face. For years the women didn't speak without yelling, until finally something happened—though Lila didn't know what—and they made up, all that anger forgotten.

So maybe AJ&P wasn't a good topic either. Lila wracked her brain for what to say, when Annie blurted, "He decided he didn't want to be serious, you see. We're in our sixties, knocking on death's door, but by God, be sure to keep your options open!"

"Ohhh," Lila said, treading carefully. So far, she had lived at Annie's for a week, and she and Marty had been on and off again twice. Which was one of the reasons she had added Annie to her to-do list. But if she said something bad about Marty and they made up, Annie could be angry that Lila spoke out against him. Which all meant Lila was in a lose-lose situation here. If she said nothing, Annie would think she was taking Marty's side. If she said something, then she could be resented later.

Taking her time at the Keurig, she placed her K-Cup into its spot, then her coffee cup, then hit the right size and waited, careful to keep her back to Annie.

"Well? Are you going to tell me what you think or aren't you? I didn't come over here to watch you make coffee."

Jesus take the wheel.

Lila closed her eyes and turned around slowly, careful to watch each word she said for fear of being misinterpreted and becoming, in turn, homeless. "I don't know. I'm not exactly a poster child for dating or men, Ms. Annie. But I'd say you need to take care of you. If he doesn't want to be with you, as amazing as you are, then he doesn't deserve you. Maybe you should move on. But then again, Marty seems like a nice man, so perhaps you should talk to him. See if y'all can't work it out."

The TV was on in the family room, the news talking about the latest election. Good God, how long had this woman been in her apartment? Lila tried to push aside how badly that creeped her out. Ms. Annie wasn't a stalker. She was just nosy . . . and maybe a tad crazy.

Stalling, Lila went to work adding sugar and cream to her coffee, then took a sip, wishing Annie would let her get a solid cup in before throwing this stuff at her. Finally, she smiled at Annie. She thought maybe everything was fine, when Annie cleaned up her paper, plucked a muffin from the plate, and took a bite, then around a mouthful said, "You're right." Lila released a relieved breath. Thank God, she— "You aren't good at giving dating advice." Then Annie walked out, and Lila burst out laughing. Wow, just . . . wow. Her sanity may not survive her living there!

Taking her own muffin, she went over to the couch and sat down, took a bite, then moaned loudly. *Damn, this is sinful.* Annie might be crazy, but she sure could cook. She downed the last of her coffee and stood to grab more, when a story on the news grabbed her attention. The words MISSING PERSON IN CHARLOTTE flashed on the screen, each letter hitting Lila like a punch to the chest. Suddenly, all the air was sucked from her lungs, the words stealing the comfort she'd felt before and replacing it with fear.

It couldn't be. No, because that would mean . . .

Lila slid the remote off the coffee table and fumbled with it until she found the volume, then hit the arrow several times until she could hear the news story clearly.

"The family of local student Elena Campbell is asking your assistance in finding their daughter." A photo of a dark-haired girl with large blue eyes and a bright smile on her face appeared on the screen.

She was young, pretty, the sort of girl who had her whole life before her. "Twenty-two-year-old Elena disappeared on Friday, April 14, at approximately ten a.m. while on her morning jog. Elena is a nursing student at UNC-Charlotte, set to graduate this May. If you have any information regarding this disappearance, please contact the number at the bottom of the screen or your local police station."

The news anchor switched to another story, but Lila wasn't listening. Another girl had gone missing in Charlotte. This was the first report of anything like this since . . .

No. I'm not going there. I won't think about that now.

Lila slumped down on the couch as goose bumps worked through her. He'd gotten off. Our legal system let a madman loose, and now he could be at it again. What if he didn't release Elena? What if the police couldn't get to her first? What if . . . ?

She drew a rattled breath to try to calm down, but it was no use. Her pulse was racing, her heart hammering in her chest, her thoughts on a million things she'd promised herself she would no longer think about.

Unable to just sit there, Lila grabbed her cell and hit her lawyer's number, but then she realized the office wasn't open yet. Frustrated, she ended the call and tossed her cell phone on the couch, anger and fear working through her in even turns.

She thought about everything the news story had said. Maybe this was a different situation. Maybe Elena simply needed a break from her life, and her parents were freaking out because she hadn't called them in a day. Maybe this wasn't a repeat attack. But even as she tried to convince herself that everything was okay, she couldn't get her heartbeat to slow down or force her hands to stop shaking.

Because it might be a misunderstanding, but there could also be a girl out there, petrified and tied up, while she waited for help . . . that would never come.

"Tracy, can you grab me some more towels?" Lila called as she stared down at the disaster before her and cringed. "And maybe a mop?"

The one good thing about going to work was that it kept her mind off the news story she had heard earlier. The bad thing? She was now cleaning up a Great Dane's vomit.

It had been a week since Lila started, and though she wasn't allowed to actually treat any of the animals, she was allowed to clean up their messes. Case in point, the current horror before her. The Great Dane was white with black spots and patches, affectionately named Oreo, and he was a beautiful dog. A beautiful giant dog. And he was about three times larger than his owner, Ms. Lockley, a petite older lady who couldn't weigh a hundred pounds. So when Oreo received his first booster shot, he tore through the exam room, knocking over everything in his wake.

Screams erupted throughout the animal hospital, followed by barking by every single dog in the place, including Oreo, though it was less of a bark and more of a howl. It took Baxter and Lila twenty minutes to grab the dog and calm him down, but it was too late by that point. Oreo the Tornado had struck, and the exam room and everything in it was torn and broken and generally destroyed even before Oreo decided to vomit all over the floor—likely as sickened by the whole encounter as the rest of them.

Immediately, Baxter took Ms. Lockley and helped her and Oreo to another room to finish the exam, and then shot Lila a look over his round glasses, for which really the word *spectacles* was a better fit, and said, "You can clean this up, while I finish with Oreo in the next room." And then without even waiting to ask if she was okay with that, he closed the door and she was alone to stare at the mess.

Now, Lila was a worker. She would never shy away from work, never push something off on someone else that she could do, but she hadn't suffered through eight years of education—okay nine, because her first year of undergrad she hadn't been sure what she wanted to do and changed her major three times—to scrub floors. And Baxter's unwillingness to let her do anything that hinted at real medicine was starting to grate on her nerves.

She had just pushed out of the exam room door to grab even more towels because the five Tracy had given her hadn't made a dent in this mess when she narrowly missed slamming into Charlie.

"Hey, Speed Racer," he said, gripping her elbow to help balance her. "Where you going in such a hurry? Off to save the world, one animal at a time?"

And just like that, Lila's lip quivered and she fought back the surge of tears that refused to go away. Dang emotions. Dang tears. "No, because apparently I'm not a real vet. I'm a janitor." She pushed open the exam room door and motioned to the massive mess, and

Charlie started to laugh before catching her glare and clearing his throat instead.

"Baxter get in a fight with himself again?"

Her mouth quirked up. That was the thing about Charlie—he could always make her smile, even in the most horrific of situations. Like Lucas getting deployed. Or Oreo the Tornado wreaking havoc on exam room 3.

"Now, let's see what kind of mess you got in there."

Charlie pushed into the exam room like he owned the place. And just like everyone else who knew the man, Lila could do little else but follow after him. His hands went to his narrow hips, and Lila caught for the first time how he was dressed—cargo shorts and a fitted Black Crows T-shirt that looked like he'd had it since he was a teenager. On his feet were a different pair of flip-flops, and she couldn't help grinning down at them when he glanced over at her.

"What?" he asked, eyeing his feet.

"How many pairs of those do you have? I've seen you three times now and every time you've had on a different color of those same flip-flops." She cocked an eyebrow at him.

"So?"

"So, aren't guys supposed to own only one pair of each kind of shoe, and even those are about a hundred years old, holes in them, and falling apart?"

Charlie lifted a fallen shelf and rested it back against the wall, his bicep flexing in the effort, and Lila found her eyes trained there, her ability to swallow coming into question.

"Now, I don't know what kind of dude you've been hanging around, but us classy folk"—he pointed at himself—"prefer the finer things."

Lila giggled, each second around Charlie easing the knot in her stomach. It was so easy to be around him, like breathing, everything about it comfortable. "Like a twenty-year-old T-shirt? And Havaianas flip-flops?"

"Hey, a man likes what he likes, woman. And I like these flip-flops. Jade got me hooked on them back at my days in the Keys, and I can't find another pair that works quite as well as these."

"Jade?"

"Huh?" He was by the back wall now, trying to organize the medical equipment that had been strewn across the floor and looking at each thing like he wasn't entirely convinced it should be used on a living thing.

"You said 'Jade.' "

His hand paused midway to a bag of spilled dog treats. "No, I didn't."

"You did. You said 'Jade.' Who's Jade?" she asked. And was it her imagination or had the air changed in the room and Charlie gone super rigid?

"No one. Look, want me to send someone to help clean this up? I kind of needed to talk to Baxter. Vet thing."

Lila's heart dropped. "Right. Of course." A vet thing—so obviously he'd need Baxter, not her. She fumbled with her own T-shirt, a Crestler's Key Animal Hospital one, apparently the dress code for Mondays and Fridays and any other day when Baxter decided he wanted the staff to match. Of course, he didn't wear the shirt.

Charlie closed his eyes and shook his head. "Damn, I'm sorry. My mouth got away with me there, and I don't like to . . . Never mind. Listen, I hate to leave you hanging here, but I promised Zac and Brady I'd meet them at the shop, and Zac's never late, so . . ."

"It's okay. I can give Baxter a message for you. What is it?"

He ran his hands over his face and peered back at Lila, clearly feeling guilty. "I really am sorry. In fact . . ." He snapped his fingers. "Forget Baxter; you can do it."

"You're not making sense. What exactly is it that I can do?"

"We need a part-time vet at the farm. Just someone to pop by and make sure all the animals are looking okay, doing their thing. Zac wanted me to ask Baxter if he was up to it, but why don't you do it instead?"

Lila waved her hands through the air. "Oh, no."

"Why?"

"Um, because Baxter won't let me do anything other than clean up animal feces. He sure as heck won't let me tend to your animals."

Charlie smirked. "See, you're forgetting a very important detail here."

"Which is . . . ?"

"Baxter doesn't own Littleton Farms."

Lila smiled. "No, he doesn't. I hear a trio of reckless men do."

"You'd be right, and the center of that trio is none other than this hot thing in front of you right now. So, it's done." He pointed at her.

"Congrats you got the job. Come by the farm when you get off, and I'll introduce you to the rest of the staff."

"But Charlie . . ."

"*Shh*, woman. I said it's done. Now—shit." He stared at his watch and then Lila. "Gotta run or Zac's gonna be on my case. See you around six, Tiny Girl."

"Lila."

He winked. "That's what I said."

And then he left and Lila turned back to the mess before her, but instead of the defeat she'd felt moments before, there was a tiny bit of hope, and for once, she loved the word *tiny*.

Chapter Six

What *the hell had just happened?*

Charlie shut his truck door and pressed his forehead to the wheel, trying to make sense of things. Why had he said Jade's name? Why of all slips of the tongue did he have to go there? It was like his walls went down around Lila, and he stopped trying so hard every second of the day. He hadn't realized before that moment how hard he worked to be normal, how he pushed away the bitterness that clawed at his insides and forced a smile instead. Even around his own family. It was exhausting.

But with Lila, everything was easy, and in turn everything in him became centered.

Up until he thought about how his body kept reacting to her and that summer-and-wildflowers scent of hers. Or what Lucas would say if he knew Charlie's real thoughts about Lila. And suddenly there was nothing easy about it. But Lucas had been crystal clear—don't touch his sister—and Charlie respected his friend too much to do anything other than honor his wishes.

His phone vibrated against the cup holder, and he spied Zac's name before accepting the call. "Almost there."

"We've been waiting for—"

"I know. Problem at Baxter's."

"Does that problem go by the name *Lila*?" Brady called, and Charlie cursed Zac for forever using speaker.

"Can't you ever just hold the damn phone? Is it really that heavy for you? What lazy-ass uses speaker all the damn time?"

The sound of shuffling filled the void, and then Zac's voice. "This lazy-ass. Now hurry up." And then the phone went dead.

Bastard.

Well, he'd done it now. Charlie would take his sweet-ass time, stalling at every stop sign and traffic light. Even if there were only two stop signs and one traffic light, and that one was forever flashing.

The streets were clear for early afternoon, the sky so blue he'd bet half the town was outside tending to their yards while their kids rode their bikes or threw a ball around. Another month and sprinklers would be running, squeals calling as those same kids ran through the water. It was typical spring in Crestler's Key. Only suddenly all the things Charlie liked to do—camping, hiking, fishing—no longer seemed so fun. They seemed . . . lonely.

Which made him think he should invite someone to go with him, but every time he thought about asking someone, the only name that came to mind was Lila's. The very person he'd been instructed to stay away from. But then hadn't Lucas asked Charlie to protect her, to look out for her? Didn't that mean he needed to spend time with her, check in on her?

Yes, yes it did.

An idea came to him as he parked around back of Southern Dive and threw his keys in the air, catching them easily, excitement building in his chest. Because suddenly Lila wasn't the forbidden fruit that he craved but wasn't allowed to sample. Oh no, he was supposed to be around her. And even if they remained purely platonic, it made him feel a contentment inside that he hadn't felt in a long, long time.

He just had to keep it platonic. Which he could do. Hopefully.

"Dude," Brady called as soon as Charlie stepped foot inside the shop. "I thought we agreed that you would show us your designs before you posted them on Instagram to your admirers."

Shit. Not this again.

Charlie continued on around the counter and dropped his keys in the small clay bowl Carrie-Anne, Zac's daughter from his previous marriage, had made him in art class last year. "Spontaneous thing."

"Nothing you do is spontaneous," Brady said. "You just like them better than you like us."

Zac laughed. "Pretty sure he likes anyone better than he likes you."

Charlie nodded to his brother. "Nice one."

"I try," Zac said. "So, on last month's numbers, I think—"

"How many followers do you have now, anyway?" Brady asked, not giving up yet.

Charlie hadn't figured out if his brother's relentless attention to his designs was brotherly support or what, but he was getting tired of answering questions.

Brady huffed, impatient. "Waiting here."

Again he tried to shake off the conversation. The Instagram thing was another Jade creation in his life, and one that he would have been happy to close down if it weren't for all his followers and how supportive they had all been when he'd decided to open Southern Dive. Five followers wouldn't have been a big deal, even a hundred, but his list had become ridiculous even by Instagram standards.

Originally, Jade would post pictures of him doing his thing. Diving. In a wet suit. Anything and everything to capture him shirtless, and because he was a twenty-something dipshit, he let her. It had surprised him at first how quickly his follower count grew, and he feared once the pictures of him doing nothing but standing there with his shirt off were gone, the followers would die off. But then he started posting cool shit. Pictures from especially dangerous dives. Or ghost ships deep down in the ocean, long since forgotten. Fishing trips and large kings. Shark fishing from the shore.

Eventually, his "let me show my pecs" Instagram account morphed into "let me show you my latest adventure," and boy did his follower count soar. It took him a while to realize that they wanted a story. They wanted to come to his page and not just see a cool pic, but read about it, experience it. So he offered as much detail as he could manage.

When he moved back to Crestler's Key, the followers went with him, interested in this new life of his—running a dive shop, taking people on check-out dives, lessons, and then the farm. Hell if they didn't love the farm.

So it made sense when he started playing around with the T-shirt designs, he would post them to his followers first. For a crowd of nearly four hundred thousand, they were surprisingly supportive. More so, at times, than his two brothers. Who were both watching him now.

"I don't know."

"You do," Zac said, setting down a box. "And it's awesome. Keeps the online orders coming each week. So you talk your talk and do your thing. This one's just jealous he don't have a tenth of your following."

Brady scowled, but it was true. He was the social one of the brothers, Zac erring on the quiet-confidence side, and Charlie too laid-back to be overly social. But all that changed on Instagram, and he'd been offered countless ad deals because of it.

For now, the only ads flashing around that had anything at all to do with him were for Southern Dive. Of course, if he actually manned up and started the T-shirt business, he'd have to rethink his less-is-more approach to marketing.

"Seriously though," Zac said as he unpacked the inventory, "what design?"

Every Monday they met at the shop to talk about sales from the previous week, unpack the deliveries for that day, and often it was the only chance they had to be brothers without the town or family or women around to distract them. Charlie missed his brothers, even though he saw them all the time. Seeing them wasn't the same as knowing them, and he wasn't sure he knew them anymore. Really knew them. Not like they used to know each other when they were younger.

Knowing they wouldn't shut up, he reached into his pocket for his phone, clicked his photos, and tapped the picture he'd taken of his latest design.

He'd been playing around with logos and themes. T-shirts like Salt Life, and Simply Southern for women, were distinctive. If he hoped to be successful, he needed a look all his own.

"The one you saw wasn't my latest. This is." He passed the phone over to Zac and tried to ignore his brothers' reactions, but there was no ignoring their excitement.

"Holy shit," Brady said, plucking the phone from Zac's hand. "Where'd you learn to draw like that? From one of those Instagram groupies?"

"Sure as hell not from you," Charlie said, swiping the phone back and shoving it into his pocket. Not for the first time, he regretted telling his brothers about the Instagram account and his small walk with fame there, but too many people had popped into the store because of it, talking about how they loved his page and couldn't believe they were meeting him in real life. A few even asked for his autograph, which had taken him the better part of a year to live down.

"Hey, I can draw," Brady said with mock offense.

"Yeah, your own name maybe," Charlie fired back, which resulted in Brady tossing a new Salt Life shirt at him and Charlie throwing it back, because clearly they were still idiotic boys instead of men.

Like always, Zac intervened. "Stop that shit. We have twelve boxes to go through, tag, and get on the shelves and racks. No time for you two fighting over nothing. Brady—he can draw and he's more popular than you. Deal with it. Charlie—Brady is . . . well, we're still trying to figure it out, but he's bound to be good at something."

Brady tossed the shirt at Zac now, who snatched it in the air, and another fight was about to brew when Charlie's cell rang loudly and he all but fell on the floor trying to wiggle it out of his pocket.

"What are you *doing*?" Brady asked, clearly disturbed.

"Answering my phone, asshole."

"Looked to me like you were having a seizure. But by all means, answer the call. Let us hear who you're hoping is calling. I think I have a guess." He waggled his eyebrows, and Charlie contemplated ways to singe those things off in his sleep.

Finally, he glanced down at the phone, and sure enough, it was Lila. But how was he going to take the call here, in the quiet store, with his two brothers staring him down, all too ready to rile him the moment he ended the call. Well, they could forget that crap.

The call ended, and immediately a text popped up.

Lila: *Hey, off now. You at the shop? What time did you want to meet at the farm?*

It took everything in Charlie not to grab his keys, yell a *see ya* to his brothers, and head to the farm. But despite the fact that he was aching to see Lila again, to feel that contentment she brought him, he had to keep his head on straight about this. Lucas was half a world away, fighting for peace, and risking his neck in the effort. He'd made two requests of Charlie—protect his sister and keep his hands to himself. Surely he could honor those two small things.

"Dude, you're grinning like an idiot," Brady said, shaking his head. "It's disgusting. What does Lila need anyway that could have you grinning that big?"

"You don't even know that it's Lila."

"Um, yeah we do. She's the only one that gets you all doe-eyed." Then his own eyes went wide and a stupid smile took over his face. "Please tell me she sexted you. Love when the good girls turn out bad."

Zac threw a water bottle at him, hitting him in the head, and Brady scowled. "Hey, that hurt."

"Then stop talking like an ass," Zac said, then he focused back on Charlie. "Seriously, does she need anything?"

And here it was. Charlie had hoped to have a little more time to prep Zac on him hiring her for the farm job. It wasn't that Lila wasn't qualified, it was more than Zac preferred not to hire friends close to the family. It made it awkward when pay raises (or cuts) happened or, worse, when he needed to fire them. Plus, Charlie's focus was on Southern Dive, Zac's the farm, so it wasn't lost on him that he'd stepped on his brother's toes a little.

"Well, actually, I was meaning to talk to you about that. I kind of . . . hired her."

Zac set out a stack of shirts he'd just folded. "For the shop? Is she certified or something?"

And now Charlie really felt bad, but hell, they needed a vet and she was a vet. "No, actually, I hired her for the farm. That part-time vet job?"

Without any other sounds in the shop other than the A/C and Brady's amused laugh, time seemed to stand still. Zac turned around, like he needed a minute, before facing Charlie again, obvious annoyance on his face, but he could bring it. He might be the eldest, but they were all equal partners in each of the businesses, and he could screw himself. Charlie had every right to hire her, and she was more than qualified. Okay, maybe that had little to do with it, but still. He shouldn't need to ask Zac. Which was one of the reasons he was contemplating the T-shirt business in the first place: Finally, he'd have something again that was just his, like his diving business in the Keys. Where he didn't have to answer for his decisions, where everything required a weekly meeting. Jade might have screwed that up for him, but he was happy there for a long time.

"Okay, so let me get this straight," Zac said. "Lila moves back into town, is here a little over a week, and you hire her without talking to us to look after the animals on our farm? The animals that we count on to help keep business up? Did you even talk to Baxter?"

Charlie crossed his arms and kept his attention on his brother. He was a lot of things, but scared wasn't one of them. Even of his big brother. "No. That old man can barely see anymore, and you want him looking after our farm animals? That makes perfect sense. Why would I hire him, when I could hire Lila, young enough to come out in the middle of the night if we need her, and she has plenty of experience. What's wrong with hiring her?"

He was offended on her behalf, and it wasn't lost on him how concerning that was in light of his assurance to himself that he wouldn't allow himself to have feelings for her. Clearly, he was already emotionally tied to her, but he hoped it was more in a little-sister way. He jerked back at the thought. Okay, maybe forget the little-sister thing. Put that crap out of his mind right now.

"You know we have a policy to not hire friends. There's a reason that's in place."

Charlie stared at his brother. "Yeah, you realize we're in Crestler's Key, right? Everybody in this town has known us our entire lives. And there are only two vets, Lila and Baxter, who's knocking on seventy. You seriously would have preferred I hire the old man?"

"Yes."

Gritting his teeth, Charlie switched his gaze to Brady. As much as it killed him to do it, Brady was always the deciding vote. "You?"

"That depends. Can I hit on her without risking some harassment lawsuit because I'm technically her boss?"

Rolling his eyes, Charlie turned around and grabbed his keys. "I agreed to show her the farm, so I'm going. For now, she's our vet. Deal with it. If she screws up, I'll take the heat, and I'll be the one to let her go."

Even the thought made Charlie's insides sour. But he didn't need to worry about firing her. Lila was dedicated and driven, and she refused to fail at anything. If she agreed to help around the farm, then she would help and she would do an amazing job at it.

"Fine, but it's on you," Zac said.

"It's on me."

The brothers nodded to each other in an agreement, and then Charlie set off back to his truck, his insides already lighter, his thoughts becoming clear. He pulled out his cell, hit Lila's last text and replied with *meet you there*, and then he started down the road, his speed increasing, a wide smile on his face.

Chapter Seven

L ila couldn't stop bouncing, that wild imagination of hers getting away from her. She pictured walking with Charlie as they toured the farm, laughing and talking, and while it was a job, she couldn't get her heart to slow down. It would be the longest amount of time she'd spent with him since they were kids and maybe the longest amount of time she'd ever spent with him without Lucas around. And she couldn't wait.

Which was silly and stupid, but there it was.

She had just turned onto the main road that led to Littleton Farm when her phone rang. Quickly, she eyed the call, and all the bubbles in her stomach quickly popped. Her lawyer.

"Steve, hey," she said, her heart picking up speed now for an entirely different reason.

"How are you liking Crestler's Key?" he asked.

"It's good. Nice to be away from things."

"Right . . ."

"So, Steve, I saw the news. A disappearance? Do you think . . . ?" Lila couldn't bring herself to say his name, but she couldn't prevent his face from appearing in her mind. A shudder worked through her.

"Honestly? I don't know. Authorities are on it; the investigation seems to be top priority, but there isn't a lot to go on."

"Okay . . ." Lila tried to breathe, but the air wouldn't reach her lungs.

"Try not to worry, and remember, you're far away from all of this. If you need anything, call, okay?"

Lila nodded though he couldn't see her. "Okay, thanks."

They hung up, and Lila's grip tightened around her steering wheel. A girl was missing and they had no idea who was responsible or where she might be. The excitement she'd felt before was replaced with worry, and she wondered if she would ever be able to go an entire day without fear or worry or doubt taking over her joy. But then maybe that was everyone. Maybe every person had something hanging over them, something that threatened to take their joy. She wondered how they pushed it away, how they brought themselves back to center. For a while, she'd taken antidepressants, and they helped, but she never felt like herself when on them. Then she tried yoga and meditation. But her mind refused to settle. That was when Lucas suggested self-defense classes, and finally, she found something that helped. It empowered her, made her feel safe, in control. Alive. And only one other thing made her feel that way—or, rather, one other person. Charlie.

At the thought of him, her heart felt lighter, so when her phone rang again, and she thought it could be Charlie, she almost ran off the road trying to grab it, eager to hear his voice and feel the comfort it brought her. "Hello?"

"Hey!" Lila smiled at Audrey's voice, forever loud and filled with giddiness. "I just passed you and waved, but I don't think you saw me. Where are you headed in such a hurry? Hot date?" Audrey asked with a laugh, and Lila realized how laughable the excitement curling and swirling in her stomach was.

This was Charlie. *Char-lie.* Lucas's best friend, a boy who watched her grow up through all the embarrassment that was adolescence. There was no way that he thought about her ... the way she was thinking about him. But that ended today. No more thoughts about Charlie.

"Nowhere. Well, somewhere, but nowhere big. Charlie offered me a job at Littleton Farm as their part-time vet. I'm headed there now to check out the place and see if I want to take the job."

"Do you want it?" Audrey asked, her voice muffled now.

"Um, why does it sound like you just walked through a cloud?"

"Hold on." A ruffling sound hit her ears, before Audrey returned. "Sorry, lipstick application. Takes talent to do that while holding the wheel and the phone." She laughed.

"Lipstick? Maybe I'm the one who should be asking you where you're going. Since when do you wear lipstick at the salon?"

Audrey announced at age six that she wanted to be a hair stylist and immediately took a pair of scissors to her Barbie dolls' hair. For the next several years, every doll Audrey owned suffered at Audrey's hand, but her love for hair never went away, so she went to cosmetology school after she graduated high school, and soon became the most requested stylist in town. A smile crept across Lila's face at the memory of Audrey on her first day of work. Though they hadn't seen each other much in the last eight years, they were still the same people in a lot of ways. Audrey still experimenting with hair and makeup and clothes. Lila was still oblivious to all that mess.

"Oh, you know, since I started cutting Brady's hair. And he has an appointment with me in fifteen minutes."

"Brady?" Lila wasn't sure if she should get onto her friend for having interest in the Littleton bad boy or not. The Littletons attracted women like moths to a flame, and of the three Brady was the most likely to burn you. Plus, Audrey was the very opposite of careful when it came to her heart.

Zac and Charlie were the more mature ones, more sensitive and responsible. Brady, while not exactly irresponsible, had never cared about having a relationship. Of course, Lila had only been back in town for two weeks. Maybe he'd changed. She decided to tread carefully.

"You do remember his nickname in school, right?" Brady was in her and Audrey's grade, so they knew every rumor surrounding him, and while some were sure to be just that, rumors, others . . .

"So?" Audrey said, a hint of aggravation in her voice, and Lila contemplated keeping her mouth shut. For all of two seconds.

"So, that a guy was called *Dirty Heartbreaker* isn't concerning to you?"

"That was in high school. He's changed. We've all changed."

And that was Lila's cue to mind her own business, which she would do, so long as Brady didn't try to hurt her friend. Then she'd be in his face faster than he could flash that smirk of his.

"Plus . . ." Audrey said, pausing as she messed with something on her end again.

"More lipstick?"

"Mascara."

"Ah." Lila grinned wide. She'd have to allow Audrey to give her a makeover one of these days, but Lila was afraid she'd come away with pink hair and more eye makeup than eyes. "Just promise you'll be careful."

"Sure thing, Ms. Littleton Farms. Should be telling yourself that, don't you think?"

Yes, yes she did, but she would never admit it. "We're just friends."

"Sure you are. Anyway, gotta run. Call me later and give me the details of your hot date."

"It's a job interview."

"Riiiight." She kissed into the phone. "Love you, chat later." Then she hung up, and Lila dropped her phone into her lap and went to work tapping her steering wheel, her thoughts going back to Charlie and her decade-old crush and how very stupid it seemed to take a job with him, where that crush would be placed under the spotlight again and again. She couldn't do that to herself, and besides, she wasn't ready to be close to someone again. Not that Charlie would go there anyway.

She pulled onto the long stretch of road that led into the farm, turned into the small parking lot that Charlie had mentioned to her in a text, and parked her car. "Ugh, this is so frustrating!"

"Um, is this one of those female episodes that require men to retreat slowly for fear of getting their heads chopped off?"

Lila's cheeks burned as she glanced out her window, which she'd rolled down because she could never resist fresh air, to find Charlie grinning back at her, his light brown hair a ruffled mess, those green eyes flashing with humor. Stubble covered his jaw, and he was tan from working outside and fishing. In short, he was temptation personified, and Lila needed to find a way to resist him before she lost her mind . . . and her heart.

It was high time she come up with a game plan, a means of defense, against Charlie, and that plan began right this second.

She pushed out of her car, not bothering to take her purse or her keys, because this was Crestler's Key, and not a soul would dare steal from anyone else.

"Just damn Baxter again," she said, answering Charlie's questioning stare. She hated to lie, but what was she supposed to say? *Sorry, can't stop thinking about you, and it's freaking me out?* Yeah, no.

"Want me to kick his ass?" Charlie flashed a wicked smile that made Lila's heart dance, before she could order herself to settle down.

"He's sixty-eight!"

Charlie shrugged. "Eh, be our little secret." He winked and Lila's heart picked up speed again.

No, no, no. Defense. What was the best defense for someone so naturally flirtatious?

Then it occurred to her. Maybe she needed to throw him off his game, give him a taste of his own medicine.

"Tempting," she said, taking a step toward him, her eyes dropping. "But I can think of better things for you to do with those muscles." She gripped his bicep, and instantly, a tingly sensation moved over her, a danger sign flashing in her mind.

His mouth fell slack and his eyes darkened, and Lila had to take a step back or she might not let him go, which would be all sorts of awkward. Okay, so maybe the giving him his own medicine thing wouldn't work here. She started to release him, but her body decided to operate of its own accord, and instead of simply letting go of his arm, she trailed her hand down his bicep, over his forearm before finally separating from him.

Charlie blew out a slow breath and scratched his chin. "You're trying to kill me, aren't you?"

"What?" She wasn't listening to him. She was staring at her hand and wondering why it was so numb now.

"Nothing," he said, taking a deliberate step away from her. Awesome, now she'd officially freaked him out. "Let's get started with the tour. Then I was thinking we could do dinner after if you're up to it. Catch up. It's been a long time."

Red alert, red alert. Say no, say no!

"Sure, that sounds great." *No, no, no.* "A girl's gotta eat, right?" She grinned. *Oh my God.* First, she stroked his arm like it was a freaking cat, then *a girl's gotta eat*? Where was her brain? Clearly, she'd forgotten it in her car.

"Well, I promised Lucas I'd look after you. Though, I'm sure Annie's shoving more food down your throat than you can handle."

Wasn't that the truth. Annie took it as her job to keep Lila's place stocked with fresh baked goods and casseroles. She said Lila needed to gain ten pounds, but if Lila wasn't careful, she'd double that in no time under Annie's roof.

"She does. Too much really, but I'll deny it if you tell her I said so."

"Secret's safe with me." Their eyes met, and once again a flutter worked through Lila's chest, refusing to settle down. Charlie's mouth set and her gaze dropped down, before returning to meet his stare. This was going to be impossible, horrible, and embarrassing, and did she mention impossible? Her brain and body refused to work together around Charlie, and what was left was some mess of a person, who acted very much like a love-struck teen girl. She needed to breathe, to remember that they were friends. Relax. "If I remember correctly, you're a steak girl, right?" Charlie asked, bringing her back to the moment. "Captain Jack's makes a mean fillet and lobster. Thought we could eat out over the water."

"That sounds an awful lot like a date. Are you . . . hitting on me?" Lila asked, a smile on her face.

He stuttered, his eyes diverting. "What? Me? No. I—"

She broke into giggles as she patted his chest. "Easy, sailor. Just joking."

"That's how it's going to be, is it? You're a doctor now, so why not give a man a heart attack?"

"I'm a vet. Not so much help on a man's heart."

He stared at her then, unblinking, his wild hair matching something in his eyes. "Ain't that the truth."

Lila swallowed hard, her own heart very noticeable in her chest, the need to say something at odds with the need to remain quiet in hopes that if she didn't speak, didn't move, or breathe he'd continue to stare at her as though she were more than his best friend's little sister.

But then a cowbell ringing brought their attention to the main barn. Though, as they neared, Lila quickly realized it wasn't used as a barn anymore.

She thought of the last time she'd been to the farm. It was Halloween and the Littletons had set up a massive event. Everyone in Crestler's Key was there, and even people from neighboring towns were pouring in.

Charlie's mama had decorated with lanterns and pumpkins. They had the cornfield cut into a maze, and even had s'mores-making stations for the kids. It was magical, a perfect starry night overhead without a single cloud to hide their glow, and Lila had decided that was the day—the day she would finally tell Charlie that she loved him, that she'd loved him since she was eight years old and had any idea what the word meant. Loved him every single moment of every one of the eight years after that realization. Finally, she'd found the courage to tell him.

Because she could feel it, that weird change in him when he saw her. The way he'd light up and then push it back. Until one day they were alone at her house, out back in the old hammock, rocking away, laughing, and all of a sudden, the air became electric, tension snapping between them. The wind whipping through the trees had died down, and dusk had set in, lightning bugs popping all around them. The smell of honeysuckle floated in the distance, so when Lila drew her next breath it wasn't to take in Charlie, lying so still beside her. It was to smell the honeysuckle, to smell summer. But instead, she'd drawn in his scent, all earthy and so charmingly boyish that her brain had stopped working. She'd reached out a hand toward his, and instead of pushing her away, he took it. Threaded his fingers through hers, something shifting, a new understanding forming between them.

But then she found him that fateful Halloween night. It was only two days later. Two small, barely memorable days. But apparently they'd been enough for him to forget that she existed and shove his tongue down Bella Grant's throat.

Lila had cried for a week, but the hard thing about it, the part she couldn't reconcile in her heart yet her brain fully understood, was she couldn't be angry with him. Not really. So they'd held hands for a second. It wasn't the first time they'd touched, and he'd made no confession of feelings for her, no falling on his knees and making claims of love.

So why hadn't that helped the pain?

"Hey, you okay?" Charlie asked, sensing something change in Lila's demeanor. Maybe it was just him, but her light flirtation had been replaced by what appeared to be sadness. Yet what could have caused the change? He racked his brain for what he might have said, and then his gaze followed hers to the barn and he felt like an idiot for choosing to start here of all places.

He still remembered the fight he and Lucas had before the Halloween festival. All Charlie had done was hint at his feelings for Lila. It was an innocent statement, nothing overly direct, and yet his best friend for all his life had whirled around on him, and the rage in his eyes made it all perfectly clear: Lila was off limits for a guy like Charlie. A part of him wondered then if he'd been different, the mayor's son instead of the farmer's son, if that would have made a difference. Or maybe it had more to do with how different they were on paper— Lila, with her perfect, squeaky-clean record, never making less than an A, never the subject of rumors, never sitting in detention for some stupid shit or another.

In truth, Charlie couldn't blame Lucas for his reaction. He might have had the same one had Lucas not so nonchalantly asked about his own sister, Kate. But that hadn't happened and never would because Lucas was always a better person than Charlie.

So, it was with all that crammed into his brain that he walked out of his house, toward the Halloween festival, only to run into Audrey. She hadn't meant to confess Lila's plans. It was more that she wanted to warn Charlie not to hurt her, because nowhere in Audrey's mind was it possible that Charlie would reject Lila. No one would reject Lila. Just look at her. Then it occurred to him that he couldn't reject her either, not directly. He'd have to show her in a very direct way that he wasn't the guy for her, not even close.

Bella came along at the right time, tossing her hair, and Charlie took the easy route. It still held the number one spot as the shittiest thing he'd ever done in his life. But as twisted as it seemed, he did it for her, and it had worked.

Within a few weeks, she was dating some college boy in Lexington, and Charlie tucked away that inkling of hope he'd felt that day in the hammock, when no one was around to see him staring down at his best friend's sister like she and she alone was responsible for the sun rising that day.

And now, all these years later, he still found himself enamored in her presence. And still, all these years later, Lucas would deck him if he had any idea. Which he never would. But this time, Charlie would keep his friend's trust and avoid hurting Lila in the process.

"Ready to go?" he asked, wishing he could explain everything to her, say he was sorry, but any of that would only let on to the truth, and he could never reveal the truth to her. To anyone.

Her spine tightened, and she started toward the barn. "It looks like that barn's no longer in use," she said, changing the subject, even though neither had said anything out loud.

"It's not. We turned it into a storefront. Sophie's idea really. She has one at Fresh Foods, and we're always so busy at the market that it made sense to offer an option both for tours and online orders."

"Wow, online orders. I never would have guessed you'd be so cutting edge."

He shrugged. "We're trying. Surprisingly, we get a fair amount of orders. Even offer a delivery service for locals. It's working. For now." Which was always the thing with farming. What worked today may not work next month. Some of that was due to the harvest that season, but some of it was just the mood of consumers.

Lila glanced over at him. "What's Fresh Foods?"

"I'm surprised she didn't mention it. Seems to me the woman never shuts up about it. She bought a farm years ago, turned it into an organic farm, and set her sights on ruining our lives. Somewhere along the way, she and Zac took the love path, and the rest is history."

The small parking lot outside the barn was packed, and Charlie was glad he'd made the decision to have it added. Previously, people parked on the grass or wherever they could find a place, which didn't feel businesslike. The parking lot, plus the barn renovation and storefront made the whole thing appear very legit. And one thing Charlie had learned with his Instagram experiment—if you look like you know what you're doing, people believe you. If you look like a hot mess, they believe that, too.

So parking lot went in, the storefront was built, a fancy website was created, and sales took off.

"I . . . I don't know what's more surprising—Zac falling for an earthy woman, though I don't know if you could call Sophie *earthy*. She's like Elle in *Legally Blonde* on the outside and Erin Brockovich on the inside."

"Exactly," Charlie said, agreeing.

"But maybe more surprising is you jumping on the bandwagon to do the parking lot and store front and website for online ordering. That plus Southern Dive? When did the reckless boy I once knew become such a smart businessman?"

Charlie's eyes fell on Lila, and once again he found it difficult to look away. "People change, grow. Part of life, I guess. Ready for this?"

Her eyebrows furrowed, but then he opened the door cut into the barn door, and immediately they were met with shrills.

"Lila Jacobs! Is that you?"

Lila's face lit and she separated from Charlie to go hug his mom, Julie, who had always loved Lila like one of her own daughters. With three boys, she probably wished once they were all teens she had another daughter to balance out all the testosterone in the house. And they were all completely different. Except for their love for this farm. That much was ingrained in them from the beginning.

Julie Littleton was five foot even and received countless jokes about it from the boys, but she was always the strong mom who wouldn't put up with much. Today she wore an easy cotton dress with a Littleton Farms apron over it, her white hair styled in a short bob.

Charlie fell back as Lila followed after his mom. Julie Littleton never wore makeup, but she didn't really need to. Even in her early sixties, she glowed, her cheeks always rosy and her green eyes—the same as Charlie's—always sparkled. But they were especially bright right now as she walked around and introduced Lila to the rest of the staff who worked the store. Lila seemed to have an impact on everyone they talked to, and even though these people were strangers to her, Lila reached down to hug every one of them. Even Ed, the farm's refuses-to-retire packager for online orders who never smiled at anyone, maybe had never smiled a day in his life, was grinning like a fool at Lila.

"You look busy," Lila said, glancing around at the crowded tables, and she was right. They did look busy.

"We just received a massive order, so it's all hands on deck to get it out on time." Julie motioned to the people around them, and just like that, Lila walked around to the backside of the table.

"Where do you need me?" she asked.

"Oh, honey, don't bother yourself. We'll get it out," Julie said.

But Lila wasn't having any part of that. "I'm here and you need help. Let me help."

Julie smiled. "You always were sweeter than sugar. Well, all right then, you can help fill boxes."

"I'm on it."

Charlie crossed his arms and watched her, the way she moved, the way she so effortlessly joined the crew, them instantly trusting her. Resisting this woman might be the greatest challenge of his life.

"What are you staring at?" Lila called to him with a grin. "Afraid to get your hands dirty?"

He laughed. "We're supposed to be showing you the farm. Or did you forget that, as a vet, your job is to treat animals, not package fruit and vegetables?"

She continued boxing, finding a rhythm. "There's time for that later, right? Ed said this order has to make the FedEx pickup. Can't we help? You can hire me later." She winked and went back to work, and Charlie wondered if he'd ever met someone more selfless and kind in his life.

"Sure, we can stay. Maybe I'll hire you out here instead. Fifteen dollars an hour work for you?" he asked, jokingly.

Mom waved her hand through the air. "Ignore that boy. You're with the real boss now. Feel free to tell him to do whatever you want him to do. I give you full permission." She elbowed Charlie, and he couldn't help feeling that in two minutes flat he'd gone from having one boss in the room, Mom, to two: Mom and Lila.

"You know, this might not be such a good idea after all. Who's the order for anyway?"

Ed checked the work ticket, then glanced back at Charlie. "Children's hospital in Lexington."

"Oh, I heard about that," Lila said. "They're having a parents' day, where the parents of patients at the hospital get to enjoy a fun day with their children. They've hired a lot of entertainment, bands, balloon makers, you name it. This is so sweet of y'all to donate to the cause."

"Actually, the hospital is paying for this," Ed said, with obvious distain.

"Not anymore." Charlie went over to the order, made note of the invoice number on the job, and pulled out a pen and wrote in large letters *Paid* beside the address and contact information for the address. That would be enough to cause accounting to flag the order, and then he could call them tomorrow to discuss treating the order as a donation instead. He wished he'd known about the order when it was placed; he would have requested they "no charge" it then. It spoke to how separated he was from this side of the business, and he wondered if Zac and Brady were equally distracted. Likely so. Neither of them would take money from the children's hospital for anything they needed, let alone something like this intended to help the parents who carried more stress and worry daily than most people saw in a lifetime.

Lila met his gaze as he went back to the assembly line they'd created for the project, table after table of boxes and packaging supplies, pre-wrapped fruits and vegetables with labels boasting *Littleton Farms*. "Where do you want me, boss?" he asked with a smile.

"Right here," she said. "With me."

Chapter Eight

The smell of fresh fruit and spices hovered in the air while busy hands worked in silence completing the order. Lila took in the amazing man beside her, and her heart swelled with pride.

It was like they were teenagers again, and Charlie was the school jock who had accidentally revealed that he wasn't so single-minded after all.

Back then, Charlie's kind side had made an appearance because a freshman, Jarrett Lockton, was getting bullied for coming out. Charlie, a senior, walked over and draped his arm around Jarrett and told the crowd they could either stand there and watch Charlie and Jarrett getting their groove on or they could leave.

No one messed with Jarrett again, and somehow claiming he was gay to help out Jarrett did wonders for his popularity with the opposite sex. Every girl at the school wanted him, including Lila. Though that wasn't news by that point. And it wasn't like Charlie was looking at her anyway. He'd sooner look at Jarrett. But Lila never forgot the swell in her chest as Charlie pushed through the crowd, determination on his face as he told them to get lost.

It was the same face he wore when he walked over to Ed and announced the children's hospital wouldn't be paying their bill, even though they were boxing hundreds of fruits and veggies, and likely, the farm could use the money. Still, Charlie hadn't batted an eye, hadn't blinked, hadn't even asked how much the hospital had ordered. His generous heart didn't care.

"What are you grinning at?" he asked, bumping her elbow with his, causing a spark to ignite under her skin, and she wished she could ask him to do it again to see if the feeling would spread. It was dangerous to crave these feelings, but she couldn't argue with how good it felt to be around someone she trusted so much. The attraction was one thing, but it was more than that with Charlie.

"And there it is again," he said, pointing at her smile. "Are you going to make me guess?"

With a shrug, Lila tried to hide her face as she bent over the box in front of her to check its contents. "You're just nice. That's all."

"Nice."

"Very," she said, returning to face him, but she'd misjudged her turn. Instead of being a good foot apart, like moments before, now no more than a few inches separated them. Lila tried to breathe as her gaze met his, but with the close distance and that spicy man smell of his and the look in his eyes that said he was thinking thoughts that might, just maybe, mirror hers, the breath caught in her lungs and instead she stared.

"You're pretty nice yourself." And then he reached up and gently pressed his forefinger to her cheek and then held it out for her. She reared back in confusion. "Eyelash. Make a wish."

"I don't believe in wishes," she said, the words coming out before she could remember that this sort of Debbie-downer thinking wasn't allowed in Crestler's Key, with their forever smiles and happy demeanor.

But instead of Charlie correcting her or cracking a joke, he focused back on the eyelash, drew a slow breath and released it even slower, the eyelash blowing away. "Me neither, but maybe it's time we start believing in them. Seems a shame not to believe in something."

And Lila wasn't sure why, but tears sprung to her eyes too fast for her to blink them away. She tried to swallow back the hurt climbing inside her, the fear that had rested over her heart, and thought about the way one encounter, one single encounter, could change her so completely. Because she used to believe in wishes and dreams, promises and futures. But life taught her the hard way that living in a dream world could land you on your face, your wrists and legs bound with rope, and no hope of surviving the night.

Lila fought against the memory, the goose bumps spreading across her skin despite the warmth inside the shop.

"Hey . . ." Charlie reached out to her, but she waved him off.

"Can I just . . ." She swiped a fallen tear away and walked out, leaving everyone staring after her. Oh, what a foolish woman she was!

Breaking down after these people had been so nice to her, after Charlie had been so nice. But somehow, remembering what it felt like to dream and live, to not look over her shoulder, brought on a sadness so intense that she couldn't push it away. Because that blissful naiveté she'd felt before may never exist for her again.

She closed the storefront's door and shook out her hands. "Stupid, stupid, stupid. Just calm down. Breathe," she told herself, but that all-encompassing sadness had taken hold, and she feared that if she didn't get out of there, and fast, they might never invite her back.

So, instead of risking them seeing her, she took off for her car, slipped inside, and started backing away, ignoring the calls from Charlie as he started up the hill to where they'd parked, his form growing smaller and smaller as she drove away.

Chapter Nine

Charlie kept going around and around in his head over what had happened at the farm, what he had said, what the others had said, and still he couldn't make head or tails of it or why Lila had bolted without a backward glance. And now, he was torn—go see her or leave her alone to figure it out? He'd driven halfway to Annie's only to turn back, then turn around again, and then pull over on the side of the road. Finally, he told himself to stop being an idiot and just go. If she didn't want to see him, then he'd leave. But maybe she did . . .

"All right, man, let's see what you got," Charlie said to himself. Because apparently he was talking to himself now. Damn, it sucked not having friends around that he could talk all this shit out with. He had his brothers, sure, but Zac and Brady were . . . he wasn't sure, exactly. But not the kind of brothers you could unload on. Especially with a problem like this one.

He put the truck in park and stared up at the apartment over Annie's detached garage, a strange flutter picking up in his chest.

"God, you look nervous."

A smile split his face as he glanced out the passenger side window and then rolled it down.

Annie stood out on the front porch with her hands on her hips. The wood of the porch was stained to match the cedar siding of the house and detached garage; glossy white trim and a red door with stonework around it completed the house's exterior. The garage boasted two doghouse windows with window boxes full of colorful flowers below each, and as Charlie stepped out of his truck and glanced up, he caught sight of Lila through one of the apartment's windows, her hand raised as she held back a curtain panel.

And now his stupid heart did that galloping thing in his chest again. He was in trouble.

"Now you're staring at her. Don't you have any game at all?" Annie started forward, and he couldn't help grinning wide at her. With anyone else, he might put them in their place, but Annie was born without a filter. She wasn't changing anytime soon.

"How are you doing today, Ms. Annie?"

"I think you should have brought flowers. Lila seems like a flowers kind of girl. Or maybe you could buy her a pie. Maybe from that amazing AJ&P Bakery downtown. I hear it's good." She winked, and Charlie laughed out loud, until he heard the apartment's screen door rap shut, and now he was staring again. Embarrassingly so. But damn, this woman in the sunlight was a sight to be seen.

Lila took her time walking down the stairs that ran from her apartment door down the right-hand side of the garage. "Um, hey," she said, not looking at him. In fact, she was looking at Annie. And in that way that said she wanted her landlord to rescue her from Charlie. He needed to fix whatever had happened back at the farm, and fast, before he lost the best friend he had in town. Because, attraction or not, Lila was his friend, and he was hers, and right now, he got the feeling she needed a solid friend's ear. No judgment, no offerings of opinions that she didn't really want to hear. Just an honest ear.

"Well, see, I heard that Captain Jack's was having a special on surf and turf tonight, and since you asked me out earlier, I thought—"

Her head whipped toward him. "What? Are you crazy? I didn't ask you out. You asked me out."

He had to bite back a grin. He tilted his head, enjoying himself. "Now, that's not the version of the story I remember. There was you standing a few inches away from me, because you couldn't keep away. And then I said I liked steak. And then you all but begged me to go out with you tonight."

"Wow, a pretty girl like you begging?" Annie said, playing along. "I would expect better from a military family like yours." She tsked, and Charlie thought Lila was going to stomp her foot or scream.

"It was a little pathetic, Annie, if I do say so myself. But look at her." Charlie lifted his hand in her direction, those beautiful blue eyes glaring at him, her lips pressed together in an annoyed pout. He wanted to laugh, if not for fear that she'd forget that the moment of distraction would lift and she'd remember why she had been upset earlier.

"Well, aren't you a gentleman to come all the way out here to pick her up, when she was the one to ask you out. I guess you better head on if it's surf-and-turf night. Place gets crowded."

Lila blanched. "I didn't even know you were coming. I was cleaning. I'm a mess. Literally." She motioned down to her cut off jean shorts and tank top, hair in a messy something on top of her head, not a stitch of makeup on her face. God, she was beautiful.

"Darlin', if this is a mess, my heart might not survive being around you when you're trying."

A small smile played at her lips. "You have to say that because you're my brother's best friend."

"No," Charlie said, eyes locking with hers. "I shouldn't say that *because* I'm your brother's best friend."

Her head lifted and though they were already looking at one another, something had changed, like maybe somewhere in her heart she'd thought about him the way he kept thinking about her.

"So you want me to go out just like this, then?"

"Your choice, but yeah." He paused. "As long as you're wearing a bra. Otherwise, you might need to go back inside. I'd hate to give the fellas at Captain Jack's a heart attack."

A laugh burst from Lila's lips. "Wait a second. Wait. Are you telling me that you can't tell if a woman's wearing a bra or not? Seriously?"

Charlie's eyes heated, all those hidden desires inside him stirring up images in his head. Images that would give Lucas every right to deck him.

"I'm saying I can't tell if you are from here. We're standing pretty far apart. But if you'd like me to come closer, I'd be happy to inspect you further. Give you a more definitive answer."

Now her cheeks were flushed, and he'd officially gone too far. He needed to turn off his flirtation around her, but he couldn't seem to keep his mouth closed. Or his lower half in check, which seemed to cause his mouth to spew shit he shouldn't think, let alone say out loud.

"Y'all need to leave before it gets any hotter out here," Annie said, fanning herself. She started toward her door, then glanced over her shoulder. "And for the record, I am *not* wearing a bra." She winked, and then disappeared inside, leaving Charlie and Lila laughing after her.

"You ready?" he asked with a glint in his eyes.

"As I'll ever be. I'm sure there won't be anyone there I know anyway."

"Right. Nobody important."

So that hope of hitting up Captain Jack's without a crowd? Yeah, not happening.

Charlie parked by the road, the gravel parking lot to the restaurant so full people had spilled over to the street. Music blared out from inside, and he was tempted to suggest they go somewhere else, but this was Crestler's Key. Most places shut down at six, and as far as a steak and a decent beer, there was no better place than Jack's.

"This all right? Looks a little crowded, and we never did finalize that bra talk."

She flashed him a grin. "And what exactly were you wanting to know about my bra?"

Suddenly his throat dried up. When was he going to learn that Lila played the game better than him?

"Right, no more bra talk." He pushed out of the truck. "And I need a beer, stat." Lila laughed and he smiled over at her. "You keep me on my toes, you know that?"

"You do me, too," she said, her tone light.

This was going to be fun, just two old friends catching up . . . and not checking each other out. Because that would be wrong, way wrong. He peered over at her, gaze travelling down her, before he cleared his throat and ordered his eyes to focus on the path ahead. And there went the no-checking-out thing.

The night was peaceful, clear and perfect, the lake behind Captain Jack's calm, though Charlie wasn't sure if they would be able to grab a table out back, not with what appeared to be half of Kentucky there to hear the band and eat.

He held open the door and the cacophony when they walked up was nothing compared to inside. Music blasted out from the band that Brantley, the owner, had set up against the left-hand wall of windows, all the tables that were normally there removed to make room for the small stage.

On instinct, Charlie placed his hand on Lila's back and leaned into her ear so she could hear him over the crowd and the band. "Want to try for outside?"

"Sure, whatever is fine."

But immediately a squeal came from their right, and Audrey rushed up, followed by Sophie, and it didn't take much for Charlie to find their table. Zac and Brady were there and a few of the other guys he should consider friends and, for all intents and purposes he guessed they were. Or at least typical small-town friendships, where they all knew everything about each other.

"Hey, brother, get on over here." Brady stood up and waved for him to come to their table. "We were just wondering where you were. Should have guessed." He switched his attention to Lila, and Charlie knew what he was thinking without his brother having to say it—if Charlie wasn't going there, then he sure as hell would. *Yeah, over my damn body.*

"We were actually planning to eat outsi—"

But Audrey had already taken Lila's hand and was dragging her to the table.

"I'm sorry," she called, and Charlie shrugged, because what was he supposed to say? This wasn't a date. This was dinner among friends, and they were eating with friends now. No big deal. So why did Charlie feel so disappointed?

He shook his head as he approached Brady. "Boy, I hope you arranged a D.D. Band's just started and already you're trashed."

Brady reached out to grasp Charlie's shoulder but missed, his hand dropping beside him instead. "Nah, man. I'm fine." Each word slurred.

Charlie glanced over at Zac as though it was all his fault. "Seriously? You know he's a sloppy drunk."

Zac shrugged. "I'll get him home."

"Hey Lila," Brady called, leaning over the table and knocking over a beer in the process. Thankfully, this wasn't Charlie's first rodeo with his brother getting drunk, so he caught the bottle just before it hit the table and spilled everywhere.

"Yes, Brady," Lila said, clearly amused that the youngest Littleton was this gone.

"Did you know our Charlie here is famous?"

Oh, shit.

She eyed him curiously. "Famous? How so?"

"See for yourself."

He pulled out his cell phone, and Charlie tried to swipe it, but Lila grabbed it first. Charlie knew without having to look what he'd find on the screen.

"I don't get it." She stared up at Brady and then Charlie. "You're on Instagram?"

"Nah, *ahhh*, not just *on* there. He's like their king, worshipping followers and all."

Charlie huffed loudly. "Shut up and sit down before you fall."

But drunks tended to conjure together, and soon Kit, one of their high school friends, piped up. "No, it's true. Dude has like half a million followers on there. They like his pecs or something. Hell, I don't know."

Now Lila's face was drawn, her focus on Brady's phone, and Charlie wished he could read her mind. "Southern Dive, so that's why your shop's called that? You . . . wow." She was scrolling through pictures, and Charlie wanted to tell her to stop, beg her to stop, but how could he get out of this now?

"It's not a big deal," he said, eyes on the band.

"And wow, he's right, you have so many followers. Do you have advertisers, too?"

"*Ahh*, yeahhh. He's a genius, didn't you know? They send him crap all the time, have offered to fly him out to test products. Like I told you, the boy's famous," Brady said, each word barely recognizable now, and Charlie contemplated decking him one good time to save them both from this drunken debacle.

But now Lila was staring at him like she was seeing him for the first time. "I never even considered that you were into social media. I mean, it makes sense for a business owner, sure, but this came first?"

"No. It was—"

"And he designs stuff, too. Look at his shit. I just told you to look at his shit." Brady broke into laughter, and Charlie glared over at his other brother, half begging, half threatening for him to come to the rescue here.

"Dude. Seriously?" Charlie asked.

"Hey," Zac said with a grin, "you are famous. Not a lie there. You should see all the people who come in the shop to meet him. Some even ask for his autograph."

Not this again. It was one time, and he would never live it down.

"Good God. Can we talk about something else?"

"Aw, Charlie's embarrassed, guys," Sophie said, chiming in. "Leave him alone. He can't help it that thousands of women follow him."

At that, Lila stared up at him. "They're all women? Huh."

"No, not all women."

Brady laughed. "Just most of them. There for the pec pictures, see."

"You going to shut him up or am I?" Charlie asked Zac, who finally relented.

"Fine, fine. Brady, let's go get everybody a round."

Everyone seemed to separate at once, a few of them going to get a closer view of the band, a few to the bathroom, until it was just the two of them alone again.

"I had no idea this was your thing," Lila said, still cycling through photos.

Charlie couldn't decide if she was saying that in a good way or a bad, but there was something more in her tone. A question she refused to ask. "It isn't my thing. Well, the designs, yeah. But not the followers, the attention. That kind of thing has never been me."

"So, then . . . you post pictures of yourself?" She glanced sideways at him, her entire demeanor changing from confident woman to innocent girl.

He scoffed. "Lord no. Back in the day, when I first started it, when I was in the Keys and pushing my diving business, then sure. There were lots of pics of me diving, returning from dives, etc. Now my followers want fishing stories, stuff going on at the farm, new products at the shops. And then the designs." He ran his thumb over his lips and looked away.

"They're good."

Their eyes locked. "You really think so?"

"Really good. I think you could sell them, create an entire line, and people would scoop them up."

He didn't know why, but her approval was everything, and with that excitement on her face, for the first time, the idea seemed plausible. "I don't know. I have the following, I think, and then stable business at Southern Dive to launch okay. But it'll take time that I don't really have, and then who knows if it's successful."

"Are you kidding? Everything you touch is a success. Remember when you decided to build the tree house on the farm? Everybody said you couldn't do it by yourself, a little ten year old, but every day you went out there, and every day you nailed up boards."

He stared at her. "You saw me working?"

"I went out there every day to watch you." She fumbled with a napkin in front of her, and Charlie reached out, covering her hand with his. Her eyes lifted.

"Nobody else has ever believed in me the way you believe in me."

"Maybe nobody else sees you the way I see you."

The moment held, the band playing a cover of "I'll Be," and Charlie couldn't help thinking there couldn't be a more perfect song for them, because hell if he wasn't her greatest fan, and the more time he spent with her, the more it seemed that maybe, just maybe, she was his greatest fan, too.

"Lila . . ."

He wanted to say something, tell her how he felt, all the thoughts rumbling around in his mind. That he was glad she was back, that he finally felt like he could breathe again, that he didn't want her to leave, that he would be her friend, her lover, whatever she wanted, but he wanted to be there for her, whatever that might mean. But before he could say any of those things, the rest of their group returned to the table.

"You lovers hold up okay without us?" Brady said.

"Yep, perfect." Lila took her drink from Audrey and drank half of it before setting it on the table and turning to face the band, her attention on anything but him.

All right, so maybe it was a good thing he hadn't said what he was thinking.

"Hey, Earth to Charlie."

He startled to find Zac snapping in front of his face. "Damn, man."

"What?" Charlie asked, aggravated.

"Just didn't realize . . ."

"Again, what?"

"That you were that gone. You need to tell him."

"Who?" Charlie asked, his frustration growing. He hated when his brother spoke in code, trying to convey something that really only he could understand. Well, he and Sophie, apparently.

"Lucas."

Oh. Maybe he wasn't speaking in code after all.

"It's nothing."

Zac took a long pull of his beer, then glanced over at Lila smiling at something Audrey was saying, and then back at Charlie, and Charlie knew without having to ask what his brother would find on his face. And it scared the shit out of him.

"I've got it under control."

"The hell you do."

When Charlie glanced back over at Lila, he found her watching him, and suddenly he realized how reckless he was behaving. He needed to talk to Lucas; even if he never acted on his feelings, he owed it to his friend to talk it out. The dude might scream at him or, worse, deck him, but at least Charlie would know he was doing the right thing.

Audrey said something else to Lila, and she returned her attention to her friend.

"I'll talk to him," Charlie said, leaning back in his chair and wishing with all his heart he could turn off these feelings he was having, or at least could hide them better.

"Sooner rather than later," Zac said.

The waitress brought around their meals, and for a while they all lost themselves in good food and good music and good friends. Finally, Audrey said she was going to get another drink and asked if Lila wanted another.

"Actually, I have to be at work early tomorrow. Mind if we head on home?" she said to Charlie, and he nodded.

"You're the driver of this thing, sweetheart. We move when you say go." He threw down some cash for the tab and then said goodbye to his brothers.

They were outside, the music more muted now as they walked through the parking lot.

"Did you mean that?"

His brow furrowed as he peered over at her. She was nervous. He could see it all over her face. "Hey, you can talk to me. You know that, right?"

She nodded, but her mouth was still firmly closed.

"Hey." He took her hand and turned her to face him. They were in the shadows now, the street lights too far away to see the expression on her face.

"I just, if I wanted . . ."

And suddenly he felt a knot rising in his throat. *No, not this. Not now.* He needed to talk to Lucas, figure out if he even stood a chance here, and it had nothing to do with whether Lila would even give him a shot. He couldn't betray his friend, wouldn't do that.

A small laugh filled the silence, and she released his hand to run her own over her face and then cupped her chin and peeked at him. "Never mind. I don't know what I was going to say."

But that wasn't the truth, and both of them knew it. She no doubt knew what she wanted to say, and he wanted her to say it. He craved it so completely that it was physically painful to remain still, inches away from her, when what he wanted to do was see if her plump lips tasted as good as they looked. Then he thought of Lucas again, fighting out there somewhere, and instead of pressing her for more, he tucked his head and motioned to the car. "We're just up there."

Why couldn't this be easier? Why couldn't they just see if this was something, and then if it was something, if it was real, they could tell Lucas together. But life didn't veer down the easy path, at least not for Charlie. He opened her car door, as much because he wanted to remain close to her as to be chivalrous, and then told himself on the walk over to the driver's side to put away his feelings, to do a better job, be a better man. Because right now, his thoughts were anything but good.

But then he slipped inside and found Lila laughing hysterically, and he thought maybe he'd misinterpreted the whole thing. "Um, do I look that ridiculous?"

"No, it's this. Us. God, we're acting like scared teenagers. I can't stand it."

"Lila—"

She faced him abruptly and placed a hand on his arm. "I know. Trust me, I know. But can't we just hang out a little, be friends?"

He released a breath, but it didn't bring any relief to the stone pressing on his heart. He needed her to say this, because he wasn't 100 percent sure he could resist her on his own, and yet . . . "Yeah, of course we're friends."

"Good. Because sometimes I think you're the only person I can talk to, and I don't want to lose that over Lucas. I mean, he said for you to look out for me, right? So we can hang out a little, do the friend thing. That's not bad, right?"

"Not at all."

"Great, then. What are you doing this weekend?"

For whatever reason, this new agreement made him feel a little better. Though he knew they couldn't act on their feelings, this conversation confirmed that he wasn't the only one suffering here.

"Camping in the mountains. Doing the hiking thing."

"You can't hike alone. Don't you know people get lost doing that?"

He shot her a dubious look.

"All right, so maybe that wouldn't happen with you. But still, you could be attacked by a bear or a mountain lion or something else mountain-y and no one would know. Which is why I should probably go with you." She chewed her thumbnail and glanced out her window before peeking back at him. "Safety and all."

He couldn't keep the smile from his face. "Now who's asking who on a date?"

"Not a date. A friend protecting another friend."

"So you think your hundred-fifteen pound body is going to protect me—six two, hundred ninety pounds of pure, cut muscle?"

She rolled her eyes. "Listen, I hate to break it to you, but I haven't been one-fifteen since I was in high school. Maybe not even then. I try not to do the scale thing—or, as I like to call them, killer of a woman's self-esteem—but I'm well over one-fifteen, that's for sure."

"Right, one-twenty then. Whatever. Still. I've got this."

Her face dropped. "So you're saying you don't want me to go?"

He started up the truck. "Oh, you're going. Just letting you know it ain't because I need your protection. It's because you're cute as hell and I like looking at you."

Shit, did he just say that?

He started to fix it, when she said, "You're not so bad yourself, sailor."

And then despite every good intention, he spent the ride back to Annie's excited for things he had no right to feel excitement over. But for two days, it would be just him and her, and right or wrong, he couldn't wait.

Chapter Ten

Lila woke before her alarm went off for the first time in her life. Of course, she told herself that it was less to do with the camping trip and seeing Charlie and more to do with her need to . . . oh, who was she kidding?

Kicking out of her covers, she went into the kitchen and turned on her Keurig, then smiled, because she couldn't seem to stop smiling. Would they sleep in the same tent together? Charlie lying beside her, wow. She wondered if he snored or if he was a heavy breather or if he was one of those people who looked like angels when they slept— peaceful, beautiful.

Okay, she wasn't even there yet and she was already fantasizing about him. This was going to get bad and fast unless she reeled in her emotions. What she needed to do was focus on the camping park and what all she would need. A sleeping bag? Sunblock? Bug spray? Trail mix? What wasn't she thinking of?

Just when she'd decided to make a list on her phone, a knock at the door pulled her attention away. Lila placed her favorite mug on the Keurig and hit the largest size, then went to the door. She opened it up without looking, expecting to find Annie on the other side, some delicious baked good in hand, but instead there was no one there. Hm. Maybe Annie went back to her house to grab something and would be back in a second.

Lila went to close the door, but the light from inside caught on the small, wooden deck off her door. Sitting there, bound by plastic and a rubber band, lay a newspaper.

Huh. She hadn't received the paper before, and she hadn't signed up for a subscription. Maybe Annie signed her up, but then it was five thirty in the morning, still dark outside. The paper delivery guy wouldn't be out for hours. Which meant someone had put it there.

With trepidation, she reached down to pick up the paper, quickly slammed the door shut and locked the doorknob and the deadbolt, and then set the paper on the kitchen counter, not willing to open it. Not yet.

Okay, calm down, she told herself. This could have been Annie last night or Marty had an extra, so he dropped it for her. It could have been there yesterday and she didn't notice.

But then she noticed the name of the paper—the *Charlotte Observer*. Not the *Crestler's Key Independent*. Not the *Lexington Herald*. The *Charlotte Observer*. There was no way that a Charlotte paper would get delivered in Kentucky unless someone specifically ordered it. Who would send her a Charlotte paper?

She reached over to smooth down the plastic, and read the headline on the front page: "Another Charlotte Woman Missing."

No, not another one. Tearing through the plastic, Lila flattened out the paper to read the article. Another woman was missing in Charlotte, this time a twenty-seven-year-old teacher, but this woman never returned home after a date. Her family didn't know the man's identity, but the police were investigating.

Two women.

Two disappearances.

Both in Charlotte.

Her blood turned to ice, each thought sucking more of the warmth from her body. Because it couldn't be a coincidence. He took those women. And someone wanted Lila to know about it, but not just any someone.

Suddenly, she couldn't breathe. Only a handful of people knew what happened to her—her lawyer, her parents, Lucas, and *him*. Neither her lawyer nor her parents would send this to her, and Lucas was halfway around the world, which meant . . .

Anger ripped through her, replacing the fear so fast she hardly recognized it. "No. No! You will not get me here. You won't!" She opened her trash and shoved the paper inside, then reached for her cell and dialed her lawyer. But again, the office wasn't open. Needing to do something, she left a message with what had happened, her fears, and then without thought, called Charlie.

The phone rang three times, and she worried he was still asleep when a groggy voice answered. "Hello?"

"Did I wake you?"

"No, this is my normal voice at five a.m."

She cringed. "I'm sorry. I can call you later."

"No, I'm up now. What's the matter?"

The words were on the tip of her tongue, right there, begging to be spoken: *Tell him. Tell him everything.* But then she thought of last night, how he talked to her, how he joked around. All of that would be gone, replaced with a constant look of worry, always on edge. So instead of saying anything about what had happened to her or the missing women or the newspaper, she said, "Just wondering what time you'd be here so I can be ready."

There was a pause on the other end. "Lila?"

"Yeah?"

"You know I'm here, right?"

Her bottom lip trembled, but she refused to break down. She wouldn't give that man the satisfaction of still affecting her. She was stronger now, able to defend herself. Lucas's suggestion that she take self-defense classes had helped tremendously, and she was still working through the moves every evening when she got home from work. She was strong, capable, unyielding.

So why did she feel so weak? "I know, thanks. See you in a while?"

Another pause. "How about I come over now?"

"No, I'm fine, really. Get some more sleep."

"You sure you're okay?"

"Fine."

They hung up, and Lila set the phone on her counter, her hands trembling because she wasn't fine. Nowhere near fine.

She walked over to her family room and began to work through her moves, needing to punch, to kick, to remember how to drop someone with a single move, and with each sequence, her breathing normalized. She might not be fine, but she would not allow herself to fall apart.

Never again.

Chapter Eleven

Two hours later, and Lila felt like herself again. She'd rationalized away the paper as a coincidence. After all, she had received the paper when she lived in Charlotte, so maybe they forwarded to her new address. Or maybe . . . well, she didn't know. But she wouldn't let this wreck her weekend.

Going back to packing, Lila glanced down at what she had so far. While Lila would never call herself an expert at camping, she'd spent her entire childhood outside. Sure, mostly chasing after Lucas and Charlie, but still, she could do the outdoors. She didn't need to wear makeup or have her hair done to feel like herself, and she was comfortable enough in hiking boots, breathable shorts, and a tank to get by. Which meant she packed light, and for the most part, was as low-maintenance as they came.

And yet as she stared at her backpack, she felt like she was missing something. She had sunblock, a first-aid kit, trail mix, water bottle, hand sanitizer. What was she missing? Something she should be thinking about, something about safety. Something . . . Hmm . . .

She walked over to her dresser and began opening each drawer just to look inside, hoping she would stumble on something that might trigger her memory. Nothing. Unsure of what to do, she continued on around her bedroom, opening drawers, until she stopped at the nightstand and a light bulb went off in her head. Opening the top drawer, she peered down at the box of condoms staring back at her.

It had been a long time since Lila had thought about getting close enough to someone to even consider sex. So when she'd confessed to Audrey over lunch the other day that she wasn't on the pill—what was the point in wasting the money?—and she didn't even own condoms, Audrey showed up at her apartment at Annie's with a plastic bag from the drugstore and a brand-new box of condoms.

"Here," she had said. "I know you said you don't need them, but you never know when love might strike. Might as well be prepared." She winked, passed over the bag, and Lila had tucked them into her nightstand, not a thought about them since, until now.

She took out the box and tapped it, then she tilted her head one way, then the other, considering. Then she read every word on the front of the box, and then flipped it over to read the back, because apparently stalling was her favorite pastime. Maybe she could just bring one just in case, but then this was Charlie. The last thing she needed around Charlie was a condom, and even if somehow a miracle happened and he did make a move, for the first time putting her and her wants on the same level as Lucas's, then surely he would have his own. Women didn't buy the condoms. Still . . .

Sliding open the top of the box, she reached in to take one out just as a voice from her doorway called, "Hey, Lila, I let myself in." She turned to see Charlie coming toward her, and all of a sudden all motor function disappeared from her body. She fumbled with the box, trying desperately to hide it, but instead she ended up tossing it into the air, the condoms inside soaring like flying saucers all over her room. Her eyes went wide, her mouth open, all of it happening in slow motion, no way to stop it, and then as if the horrible scene needed a grand finale, Charlie caught the box in his hands.

He peered down at it, and then his eyebrows threaded together, before his gaze returned to her, one eyebrow cocked in question, but what could she say? What in the world could she *possibly* say to explain this?

Charlie shook his head slowly. "Wow, I never would have guessed that Annie would be so active at her age." He bent down and started picking them up, all the while Lila felt sure her entire body had turned crimson red. "Since it's her house, I'm assuming these are hers?" He eyed her, his intent clear. He was giving her an out, and God bless him for it, because right that second Lila wanted to crawl into a hole and die.

"Um, right. Yeah . . . Annie's. I found them in the nightstand. Guess she gets it on here instead of her house." Oh my God, she did not just say that! Annie was nearly seventy, and she was talking about her hook-up preferences. She was going to hell for this, no stops, direct path to hell. "And, um . . . we probably shouldn't talk about this ever again. You know, respect for her privacy and all."

"Oh, of course. Especially since she seems to prefer—" He raised a single wrapped condom closer to his face and read, "Trojan's Double Ecstasy, which apparently lets you feel the pleasure, not the condom."

Lila covered her face with her hands. "She's never going to live this down, is she?" she asked, still under the pretense that they were talking about Annie.

"Never. Though . . ." He finished picking up the rest of the condoms and put them back into the box, then handed it over to Lila, those sinful green eyes of his darkening. "Any man worth a damn will have his own. Well, maybe not Double Ecstasy." He cracked a grin, and Lila burst into laughter. "Condoms aside, are you ready to go?"

"Yes, please." *Before I die of embarrassment.*

The two-hour ride to the campground, which Charlie claimed was one of the best spots in the Appalachians, was surprisingly peaceful. They talked about their lives up until that point, both avoiding especially personal bits that clearly neither was willing to share. The air cooled as they climbed higher up the mountain, and Lila thought she may have made a fatal mistake in forgetting to pack a jacket. But at least she had her sleeping bag for tonight, and never one to be especially cold, she felt sure she'd survive. It was just two days after all.

"So, no big relationships?" Charlie asked with a grin over at her as they closed to the end of their chat about their love lives. "Gotta admit, I thought for sure you'd be married."

She shrugged. "Hey, I'm only twenty-eight. That's not too old to meet someone. In fact, I was reading this story the other day about a couple who found each other in their eighties, neither had been married before, but they met and fell in love."

"Ah, I see. Didn't realize you were holding out for the glory years to tie the knot."

She playfully pushed him. "I didn't say *I* was waiting until I was in my eighties."

He pulled his attention from the road to look at her. "So what are you waiting for?"

"I don't know. I guess the right person. Someone who can give me all the things I want and I can give him all the things he wants."

Charlie went silent for a moment, then casually asked, "What do you want?"

Lila went still, her thoughts on what she had wanted for her life before the incident changed everything. If things were different, if she wasn't afraid and she knew she could trust the man she was with, what would she want?

"I want to get married, have a family. Maybe a dog or a few chickens. A baby goat."

He laughed. "A few chickens? A goat?"

She pointed at herself. "Vet."

"Point taken. All right, so the family thing."

"Don't you want that?" she asked, hoping her tone didn't give away how eager she was for his answer.

Charlie went quiet, and Lila wondered what he was thinking, if maybe he'd already tried the family thing and it had failed. Maybe with Jade. He'd hinted that there was a story around Jade, but Lila had never been the sort of person to pry, even if she was dying to know.

The moment drew long, and Lila thought he wasn't going to answer her, when he said, "There was a time I thought about it. I pictured buying a house together and settling down, seeing if children would work into the equation, but my plan wasn't the same as hers."

"Jade."

He tensed, his hands flexing around the steering wheel. Clearly, the conversation made him uncomfortable, and once again, Lila considered changing the subject. The last thing she wanted to do was ruin Charlie's mood before the trip had even started. "I don't like to talk about her. To anyone, really. My brothers don't know the half of it. Honestly, I've told you more than I've told anyone."

"You don't have to talk about it. You know that, right?"

"Yeah, but sometimes not talking about is worse than getting it out, you know? It's like this entire part of my life has been sitting there in the back of my mind, tucked away, but the longer it sits there, the more damage it does."

And those were maybe the truest words ever spoken. Lila wondered if he had picked up on something from her, if he knew she was holding on to a secret as well. But while she didn't know Charlie's story, she knew her own, and it wasn't just that she didn't want to talk about it. She *couldn't* talk about it. Each time she tried to get it out the result was a massive panic attack, the anxiety taking over her life for days or weeks afterward. It was so hard to come back from that darkness that she found it better to not go there in the first place. Why take the risk? What good would it do?

"I don't want to force you, but if you're open to talking about it, maybe just tell me how you met. Start slow."

Charlie took the next right turn and relaxed into his seat more. Silence replaced their easy conversation, and then Lila thought he might remain that way for the rest of the trip, when he said, "Have you ever fallen for the wrong person?"

He glanced slowly to her, and she swallowed hard, unable to say anything. Because Lila felt she'd only in her life ever fallen for one person in any real, tangible way. The gut-wrenching, can't sleep, desperate for even a moment of their time kind of way. And he was sitting beside her. To answer his question, maybe Charlie was the wrong person. In a lot of ways, people would classify him as horribly wrong. But to Lila he was everything, then and now.

"Sure, we all have, right?" she finally said, not willing to dive into her true feelings. Not yet, maybe not ever.

He blew out a breath. "Well, that was me. I had just returned from a checkout dive, and she was standing on my dock, looking like she belonged right there, in my world. Thinking back, I should have known better. No one normal knew your name before you introduced yourself. But she did. I assumed someone in town had mentioned me as the go-to for dive lessons. I guess I'll never know how she got it. Anyway, she was a master at manipulation, and soon she was spending more time on my boat than not. I was prepared to propose, bought the ring and all, when I woke up and she was gone . . . with everything I owned."

Lila gasped, her hands going to her mouth. "No."

"Yeah. If I weren't on the boat, she'd have taken that, too."

"What a bitch."

Charlie laughed and peeked over at her again. "Wow, I don't think I've ever heard you use such language, Tiny Girl. Think I'm a bad influence on you."

"No, I just don't take too well to people messing with those I care about."

She knew he was staring at her even before she looked over.

"And I'm on that list?" The way he asked it, the uncertainty there, made her wonder how much damage Jade did before saying good-bye. Surely this wasn't all about Lucas.

"You've always been on my list."

"You realize your brother would have words to say about that, right?"

"I'm a big girl now, and besides, my brother isn't here."

"No . . . he's not." He pulled down a narrow dirt road and parked the truck, a thousand unspoken words lingering in the air, but Lila couldn't decipher what any of them meant. Was he saying he agreed with his brother or that he didn't? She knew she couldn't be the only one feeling this chemistry between them.

"I'm going to go grab the tent and set up. You can wait here if you'd like."

"Nope, I'm an active protector here. I'll help."

He smiled. "All right, Ms. Protector. Let's see you put those muscles to work."

They stepped out of the truck, and instantly, Lila drew a deep breath, allowing it to seep through her. It felt like forever since she was in the mountains, breathing in the pure, mountain air. The green trees, occasional wild flowers, birds calling out their sweet melody. Everything about being there oozed relaxation and peace.

Charlie had parked them at a small campsite beside a stream, but though there were spaces for a half-dozen tents or campers, and there were grills and picnic tables set up at each spot, no one else was there. Only them.

"I see you scared off all the other campers," she called as she motioned around the empty campsite.

"It's tucked so far off the main road, no one knows it's here. Of all the times I've camped here, I've only ever ran into someone one time, but they were gone in a day and I was staying a week, so . . ."

"A week, wow. And you don't get sick of it?"

Charlie grabbed the tent from the back of the truck and paused out in the open, trees all around them, the easy sounds of the stream playing out in the distance. "I could stay here forever. It's like I can finally think, the muddled chaos in my head clearing at last. I'm sure that makes no sense."

"Perfect sense, actually." Lila wasn't sure if she could stay there forever, but she could definitely get used to a few days there a month, breathing in that clean air and forgetting there was another world out there where life kept you from remembering that living involved more than work and responsibility. Life was meant to be enjoyed, not endured.

"So who watches Henry when you're up here?"

He shrugged. "Depends. Sometimes I bring him. Other times I pay Carrie-Anne to watch him. He's with her and Zac right now."

"I bet she loves that."

"She does," he said, grinning. "Though I'm not sure if she loves Henry so much as the fifty dollars I hand her when I pick him up."

A comfortable silence fell over them as they went to work setting up the tent, creating a system, and before long, they had it up and stood back to stare at their handiwork.

"So, um, what do we do if it rains?" Lila pointed to the hole in the roof, which Charlie had repaired with some combination of a trash bag and masking tape.

"No faith in me, huh? You're looking at a professional boy scout."

"You were a Boy Scout? I don't remember that."

Charlie diverted his eyes. "Well, no. Not technically a Boy Scout. But we created our own club and learned on our own. Real boy scouts."

"Meaning, you burned something and had to figure out how to put out the fire, and then you thought it was so cool, so you had to figure out how to repeat the process?"

A grin took over his face, and Lila couldn't help thinking that no smile had ever looked better on a man. "Damn, I need to remember how well you know me. It's like hanging out with a history book of my life."

She laughed. "Hey, I don't remember everything. No one remembers *everything*." Only that wasn't true. Lila's brain filed away each memory like it was vital information, necessary for life.

His grin widened. "Sure you do. You're one of those people who can't forget a thing even if you tried, but I like it." Lila stared at him. Maybe he knew her every bit as well as she knew him. Charlie cleared his throat, breaking the connection. "Want to help me grab the rest of the stuff?"

"It's as though you've never been around a woman who was willing to help, but I know that can't be right. I know your mama, re-member?"

He cocked an eyebrow. "Yeah, but do you remember Kate? Ms. I-Have-Three-Brothers-Let-One-of-Them-Do-It?"

"I'm going to tell her you said that."

Fear crossed his face, and Lila burst out laughing. "Healthy fear of your sister, I see. Who would have guessed? You realize Kate's like five three, right? You outgrew her a long time ago."

"The tiniest ones are the most dangerous. Just look at you. Five-foot-nothing and scary as hell."

"Hey!" She started to push him, when he blocked her and flipped her around, her back to his chest, his arms around her, holding her close. It was all intended to be playful, but suddenly, Lila's body warmed, her chest buzzed.

"See," Charlie whispered, "tiny thing and yet here I am, breath-less."

He released her and went to the truck, leaving Lila staring after him. She hated when he said things like that, confusing her, but then maybe he was confused, too.

Once they had carried the cooler, food, and sleeping bags back to the tent, they climbed inside and set everything up. For a six-person tent, it was surprisingly small. Lila laid out her sleeping bag, and re-alized that no matter which way she adjusted it, she would be sleep-ing directly beside Charlie, face-to-face with all those feelings she had for him. A tingly feeling moved down her spine, and then she re-membered the condom debacle from earlier and immediately jerked upright, only to slam into Charlie.

"Whoa there, cowgirl," he said, steadying her, his hands on her arms. "It's best not to make abrupt moves. I'm afraid this old tent isn't a spring chicken. I can't guarantee if you hit it too hard that it won't collapse, and then we'll be sleeping in the truck."

"Maybe you'll be sleeping in the truck," Lila said with an easy smile. "I'll be sleeping out under the stars."

Chapter Twelve

Damn, and just like that, Charlie forgot what he was doing, lost in Lila's magnetic pull. Every time she said something like that, he found himself staring, searching her face for some hint that she was joking or saying something she thought he wanted her to say. But instead, she'd hold his gaze, her eyes sparkling, her smile so breathtaking, and he was stuck, staring and caught, and yet he couldn't look away any more than he could make himself stop having these thoughts about her.

"You're staring at me."

"You noticed."

"Hard not to, seeing as I'm looking at you while you're doing it." She laughed, but there was nothing funny about it. No, this was scary shit, the kind that could end a twenty-year-long friendship. Which he couldn't let happen. And yet . . .

He reached into the cooler for a water, just to have something to damn do, but he couldn't help but look back at her again.

Like the other night, she had her hair in a mess on top of her head, and though he'd always been a long-hair guy, he found the look unbelievably sexy on her. She wore a tank top and Columbia hiking shorts, a popular pair they sold at Southern Dive because lots of women around town wore them during the summer, when people wore as little as possible. And never once had he given those shorts a second look on anyone else. But on Lila, with her long, tanned legs ending in hiking boots, he thought she might be the most adorable person in the world, let alone Crestler's Key.

Which all led to one hard truth: He needed to talk to Lucas. And he would . . . as soon as they got back into town. For now, he was here to give her a distraction, and he intended to do just that.

"You ready?" he asked, clearing his throat and his mind in the process.

She clapped. "You're the boss. Lead me. I'm up for whatever."

"All right. I thought we'd hit the trail first. The waterfalls are beautiful this time of year, and that trail to the left up there," he said, pointing ahead, "goes past two. Three, if we go off course. But that'd take a little more time and a lot more faith." He winked. "So grab your pack and bring your super powers, Ms. Protector; we're hiking."

Charlie tried to keep quiet as they went up the trail and instead allow nature to tell its own story. Everything was in bloom, and with the stream out there and the waterfalls in the distance, the mountains became magical. But he was never one to keep his mouth shut for long, so after a while, he started pointing out landmarks, explaining this plant or that, then dove into stories of family trips the Littletons had taken over the years, too many to recount.

"Did any of you ever get lost? I can't imagine all three of you hanging around your parents the whole time," she asked.

"Actually, yeah, Brady. He'll deny it if you ask him, but this one time little brother decided to get cocky."

"Of course he did."

Charlie laughed. "Damn fool told us he knew a faster route back to the campsite and was so arrogant about it, we told him to go, then. Beat us back, and we'd give him ten bucks. An hour later and he still hadn't arrived. Angry, Dad promised Zac and me the spanking of our lives if we didn't find him immediately. So we all set out, and for a while, we were real scared. Night was starting to set in, and he was barely twelve. Mom was beside herself. But then Brady turned on his flashlight and started calling out to us. Zac heard him first, and we took off. It was probably the only time we'd willingly hugged each other as boys, but damn, I was glad to see him."

"I bet. He was always your favorite."

"What?" Charlie jerked around to look at her. They'd reached a narrow part of the trail, so he'd taken the lead. "Zac's my favorite."

"No he isn't. He's the one you pretend is your favorite, because he should be your favorite. But really it's Brady. He thinks the most like you. You know..."—she shrugged—"when he chooses to think."

Charlie turned back and took two steps before stopping again. "Nah, it's totally Zac, maybe even Kate, but not Brady."

She grinned. "Whatever you say." But he could tell by her all-knowing expression that she didn't believe him.

"I'm going to tell Zac you said that."

"Why? He'll just agree with me."

"No he won't. He'll be pissed that you didn't say it was him."

"No, he won't," Lila insisted. "He'll say he knows, and then he'll go on his way. How does everybody else know that Brady's your favorite sibling but you?"

He shook his head and faced forward again, but he wasn't so sure anymore. Brady was the fun one, sure, the one willing to do anything. But underneath all that, he was also the one who had supported Charlie's T-shirt idea from the beginning. He joked about it, but Charlie knew that was just his way of keeping it current in Charlie's mind, to keep the conversation going. And even beyond the supporting-him bit, he was never judgmental, never questioning. When push came to shove, he supported Charlie no questions asked.

"Holy shit. He *is* my favorite."

A laugh broke from behind him. "I told you."

"What else do you know about me that I don't know?"

"Come now, you don't expect me to hand over all my secrets on our first date."

He pivoted around again, a grin playing at his lips. "Date, huh?"

"A friend date."

"That's a thing?"

"It is now."

Charlie wasn't sure why, but he liked the sound of that. Adding *friend* made it feel as though he were doing nothing wrong . . . even if inside his thoughts were anything but platonic.

For the next hour they continued around the trail, stopping to look out over the world below every so often, as much to show themselves how far they'd climbed as anything else. There was a peacefulness to being around Lila that Charlie found addictive. They didn't have to talk or try too hard, put on that fake smile and pretend. It was easy, and that easiness was what had his stomach turning—in good ways and bad.

Why couldn't she be someone else's sister? Anyone else's. He found himself wondering how he would have played this if she wasn't

Lucas's sister, but in truth, he already knew the answer to that question. He would have taken her on a date, then a second, and third. Kissed her for sure, and maybe more. Suddenly his thoughts drifted to those long legs, wrapped around his waist, her hair loose around her shoulders, wearing nothing but—

"Whoa!" Charlie stumbled back, landing on his ass. "Shit."

Lila pulled him back. "You okay? You almost walked off a cliff. Didn't you hear me telling you to stop?"

Um, no. I was too busy picturing you in inappropriate positions.

Christ, this was getting bad, and though he liked to think he would have stopped before diving off the side of the mountain, he couldn't help feeling the irony. Here he was, staring at this beautiful woman, who made him laugh, who made him feel so whole, and it was like he was on a cliff, deciding whether or not to jump in headfirst or slowly retreat from the danger.

"Sorry, got distracted there."

"You think? I'd never seen you so intent. What were you thinking about?"

The image returned, her head tilted back as he kissed her— *Dammit.*

"Nothing. Nothing at all. Look, we're here." Thank God for the freaking waterfall to distract her so he could calm himself down.

They stepped up to the edge of the trail, this part with a protective railing so hikers could look out and see the waterfall. Lila gripped the railing and her mouth dropped as she took it in. It stretched from one side of the river to the other and cascaded down in white and golden waves over giant rocks, before crashing to the pool below.

"Wow, that's just . . . wow. Was that here when we were kids? I don't remember it."

"Yeah, but the trail wasn't, so you might not have hiked this far."

"But you did?"

He brushed off the awe in her voice. "We were boys, did our thing, which typically erred on the reckless side, so yeah. We've probably hiked every inch of these woods."

They fell into silence as they stared at the falls, their beauty breathtaking, something created by nature, and that part of it never failed to amaze him. But then his gaze cut to Lila, her face relaxed as she watched the falls, her chest rising and falling slowly, absorbing nature, and then she turned to look at him.

"You're staring again."

"I know," he said, his voice barely a whisper.

"Why?"

"Because you're you . . . and I can't seem to look away."

Chapter Thirteen

Okay, what did that mean?

O Goose bumps had covered Lila's skin the moment Charlie said it, and now, an hour later, they were back at the campsite and she still couldn't feel her fingers or her toes. She kept looking over at him, waiting for him to elaborate, to hint at what he meant. Or, you know, to pull her into his arms and kiss the breath out of her. Either way, she needed him to do something.

But instead, they continued on the trail, Charlie talking about this plant or that, this stream and the kinds of fish you could catch in it, and all the while, Lila had one thought and one thought alone on her mind: *Do you want me?*

Because he kept saying these things that took her breath away and then turning away and shutting down, and Lila didn't know if that meant he was attracted to her, but didn't feel anything serious, something worth risking his friendship with Lucas. Or if he had real feelings for her, tangible, all-encompassing feelings. The kind of feelings where he couldn't stop thinking about her, the way she couldn't keep her mind off him, and was battling inside his head a war over being loyal to Lucas or trying things with her because he knew this thing between them could be amazing if he'd just take a chance.

But then those were a lot of *ifs*, and surely that many *ifs* didn't equal reality.

In a way, she knew it had to be hard for him. Lucas would never be okay with her dating one of his friends. But this wasn't just any friend; this was Charlie. Charlie, a man so good he didn't even see himself clearly. Lucas had to know that Charlie was amazing, though, or he would never have asked him to look after her.

Because he was amazing. Funny and smart and kind and he made her feel so safe and—

Lila paused mid-motion. She wasn't afraid. She was setting up two folding chairs for them and a small folding table, while Charlie made dinner. And she wasn't afraid.

Here she was, in the middle of the woods, darkness surrounding them, a few lanterns Charlie had brought their only light and then the stars and moon above, and yet . . . she wasn't scared. Not even a little bit.

For six months, she had lived in a closet, closing off everyone, and being so over-the-top she bordered on obsessive, all so she wouldn't make the same mistake again. Wouldn't be so stupid.

Because that was what it all came down to—she was stupid before, and she would never allow herself to be stupid again.

So she went about her day, she woke and worked on her kickboxing and self-defense training, and then she continued on in her day, but she was always on edge. Even in Crestler's Key. Her eyes always a little wide, her back always a little too straight, always tense.

But not now.

Her gaze cut over to Charlie, who was finishing up the steak and potatoes on the grill, and before she could stop herself, her emotions took over and she blurted, "I need to know what you're doing."

He paused midway to flipping one of the steaks, and his eyebrows rose to his hairline. "Grilling . . . you know, pretty much the only option we have out here."

"Not with that," Lila spit out, aggravated now. "With me, with us. What are you doing? Why do you keep saying things that read like you want me, but then you back away? Because I gotta tell you, I've lived in a prison for six freaking months. Unable to take a step without being absolutely petrified, looking over my shoulder all the time, unable to draw a real breath. Basically, a complete and total mess except when I'm with you! And I don't know what that means, but it has to mean something, and I can't just pretend that I don't—when you and I—and this is—" Tears burned her eyes, her throat closing up, and in one move, Charlie dropped the spatula in his hand and pulled her to his chest, his arms around her.

"It's okay . . . I'm here."

She tried to fight back the sob working through her chest, but she knew it was a futile effort. Finally, she released the control she'd been holding onto so tightly, and without the weight on her shoulders, her knees buckled, her body too exhausted to try anymore. Charlie grabbed her and then before she could think or guess what he was doing, he swept her into his arms, cradling her close. He walked over to one of the foldout chairs and sat down, Lila still in his arms.

Wiping away her tears, he held her face in his hands, his eyes narrowed in concern, and she started crying all over again. Because this was exactly what a man wanted—a woman to scream at him, then cry her eyes out.

"Please, tell me what's going on," he said. "Why are you scared? Why did Lucas ask me to protect you? What happened to you? Because I swear to God, I will snap someone's neck if they hurt you. I will hunt him down this second and take him out. Just point me in the right direction and he's gone, poof. But you have to tell me, because I keep seeing you tense up and it's killing me inside. I know you, and this, this isn't you. The Lila I know is fearless."

"I used to be," Lila said, wiping away another tear.

"Until . . . ? What happened?"

Lila turned her head and noticed the grill, the steaks sizzling. "You should probably get the food off."

"And then you'll talk to me? Because I get it if you need a minute, but I think we need to talk about this."

She eyed the fire, the reds and oranges dancing, and felt the words rising up in her. "Okay."

"I'll be right back. Two seconds." Charlie stood up and set her back in the chair, then peered down at her with concern.

"I'm okay."

"No, darlin', I don't think you are."

Her lip trembled, and she glanced away from him before she lost it again.

Quickly, Charlie went to work taking the food off the grill, made two plates and returned with two beers. He set their food on the small fold-out table and moved it in front of them.

"I get it if you don't want to eat right now, but we hiked all day, and you need to refuel your body."

"See? Like that. That's exactly what I meant when I started this whole thing. Why do you care so much?"

Charlie opened his mouth, then ran a hand through his hair and sighed heavily. "All right, how about we make a deal? You tell me why you're afraid, and I'll tell you why I am."

She stared at him, his eyes locked on hers, nothing but honesty there, and she could only nod. "I'll try, but do you care if we eat first? I don't know if I'll be able to once we start talking."

Charlie opened his beer and then hers. "You and me both." He took a long pull, then a second, and she did the same, both of them needing a little liquid courage.

They dove into their food, eating in silence except for the easy sounds of the woods surrounding them. A large, full moon shined down from above them, and Lila thought maybe she could live in the mountains after all.

"I've never had potatoes and onions like this before," she said after a while.

"Family recipe. I'm surprised Lucas never made it for you."

She guffawed. "Lucas cook? He can't even boil water."

Charlie was staring at her now, but not in that longing-for-some-thing way he had earlier. Now he was waiting, trying to be patient, but he expected her to talk, and honestly, she should talk to him. She owed him an explanation for the breakdown. After all, they were friends, and he'd opened up to her. But what if she lost it again? What if she couldn't calm herself back down? She'd just started her job with Baxter a few weeks ago, and he barely tolerated her. He certainly wouldn't accept a temporary leave while she retaught herself how to cope.

He set down his plate and leaned toward her. "Look, I don't know what happened, but you look afraid. In fact, you always look a little afraid. Like you're waiting for someone to jump out, but that's not going to happen here. I can promise you that. You're completely safe."

"Completely safe? As in, no bears or as in don't worry about po-tential thieves because I'm packing?" she joked, but then she caught the expression on his face. "Oh, you are."

"Always."

"You always carry a gun?"

Charlie grabbed his beer and leaned back in his chair. "Not al-ways. I carry if I'm going to be somewhere that might warrant it. These mountains are safe, but there have been a few encounters over the years. Nothing too serious, but enough that, yeah, if I'm camping up here, I'm carrying. Especially when you agreed to come with me.

Lucas wasn't screwing around when he asked me to look out for you, and I take the job seriously. So you're safe. I can promise you that."

She nodded and tilted her head up to look at the stars, the full moon, and then slowly released a breath. "I have this friend in Charlotte who met her husband online, and they're one of those couples that are just ... meant to be, you know? They act alike and think alike, one wrong cut at the salon, and you'd confuse which is which from behind. And you know how when some people are happy, they think it's their responsibility to make everyone around them happy, too?"

"You just described half of Crestler's Key," Charlie said.

"Exactly. Well, my friend is one of those people, so I couldn't argue when she suggested I join the dating site that had brought her such joy. What was I supposed to say? So I created an account, assumed I'd ignore it, and eventually she would forget. But she didn't forget. She asked me about it every day. I'd been on a few dates up there, but nothing serious, which was as much due to my focus on work as anything else, but my friends and family were getting worried. I guess a woman in her late twenties, not married and not in a serious relationship, is a freak of nature that requires an immediate fix. God forbid a woman focus on her career."

Lila paused to take a drink of her beer, needing the alcohol to work through her and relax her enough to be able to tell the story.

"So, I signed up on the site, and really thought nothing of it, until I started getting a few messages. I'd look at their profiles, but otherwise I really just kept going, not actively engaging, until one caught my eye. His name was Wyatt Vane."

Charlie's eyebrows shot up. "Vane? As in ..."

"Yeah, the superstore. He's a senior vice president, rich and handsome. He was nice and charming. We talked several times, and then finally I got up the courage to meet him, and we clicked. He knew exactly what to say, and I was impressed with how laid-back he was in light of his wealth. We went on several dates and then—"

She took another long pull of her beer, and then fighting back the panic climbing from her stomach, decided to down the entire thing.

"And then what?" Charlie's tone had hardened, the muscles in his arms flexed from gripping the arms of his chair.

Swallowing hard, Lila focused on the stars above, on counting them until her heart slowed. "Until one night changed everything, changed me. We went out to dinner, like before. I remember eating, having a glass of wine, getting back in his car, and then the next thing I remember, I—I—"

Charlie reached over and took her hand. "I'm here. Stop if you need to."

She shook her head, fighting back the tears that burned her eyes, but there was no fighting them. "I woke up on a cold floor, like concrete, my feet and hands tied up, tape over my mouth. I was blindfolded, so I couldn't see where I was, only hear and feel. My head was clouded, like the way you feel when you wake up from a dream you thought was real. Only it wasn't a dream, it was my worst nightmare."

Charlie jerked out of his chair, standing before her, anger taking over, but he didn't say anything yet. He wanted her to continue.

"I'm not sure how long I was in that room, or whatever it was, but he would come down to see me, t-t-touch me." Charlie cursed under his breath. "It was a game to him, I think. Watch and see how afraid I'd get. He got off on it. There was a point when I thought I was gone, that he was going to kill me. But then I passed out again, and the next time I woke up, I was in my apartment. Alone. I called 911, and an ambulance picked me up. There were bruises on me and cuts from the ties around my feet and hands. The cops came to question me, and I told them everything I knew. Even though I never saw my attacker, I knew it was Wyatt. That was the one thing out of all of it that I knew for certain. A lot of the rest was a mystery. How I had gotten there, details about the place, why he put me back in my apartment. He hadn't raped me, so there was nothing, you know, there for them to use to identify him, but the cops felt my recounting of what had happened was enough to bring him in."

Charlie started pacing then, his arms crossed, his head shaking, yet still he kept quiet.

Taking a breath, Lila pulled her knees to her chest and wrapped her arms around them. "But see, this is where I learned first-hand the corruption of the legal system. Being a Vane, he has people everywhere and could afford the best defense attorney on the planet. We went to trial, but there was not enough evidence to convict him. He'd been careful not leaving a sign anywhere, making sure he had witnesses who could attest to where he was and when. He'd covered his tracks perfectly, even going as far as to have character witnesses who claimed Wyatt couldn't possibly have done this. They turned it on me, claiming I just wanted his money. But all I wanted was for him to be locked away where he couldn't hurt anyone else."

Charlie slammed to a halt and stared down at her with fire in his eyes. "Wait a second. He's not in prison?"

Lila shook her head slowly, her bottom lip trembling. "He got off, free and clear."

And that did it. Charlie kicked the grill, his anger taking over. "He kidnaps you and gets away with it? All because he's rich? Bullshit. We have to do something, appeal."

"It's not up to me. The DA's office has to decide to appeal, and there just isn't enough evidence. Either he was ridiculously careful or the police are covering for him. I tried to continue my life in Charlotte. I loved my friends there, and my job, but therapy wasn't helping. So Lucas asked that I move back to Crestler's Key. He wanted me to buy a gun and get my carry permit, like you, but I'm not as comfortable around them. And then he got deployed."

"So he asked me to look after you."

"Yes."

"I had no idea," Charlie said helplessly. And he did feel helpless. Angry, and helpless.

"I know," she said, wiping away another tear.

Charlie felt like he was having a heart attack, the anger and need to punch something so real, he was amazed he hadn't taken out his frustration on a nearby tree. But that wouldn't help Lila. Right now, she needed to remember that something happened to her. Something horrific. But it didn't define her. She was strong.

"Listen to me," he said, walking near. "You survived this."

"I survived because he wanted me to. That much is clear. He put me in my apartment. Put me there. He could have just as easily killed me. He wanted me to live so he could show me how easy it was for him to come into my world, take me, and put me back, and there wasn't a damn thing I could do about it."

Charlie squatted down in front of her, needing her to see and hear him clearly. "You're giving him too much credit and yourself too little. You are strong. Too strong to let this break you. You're back here, working, going out with friends. He didn't take anything from you. He failed. You going on with your life proves that. You didn't give up, and that was what he was hoping you would do. He did this to break you. But don't you see? He failed."

When her watery gaze hit his, Charlie thought he might break down with her. He'd never been so overwhelmed with sadness and rage in his life. Not even when Jade left. This, this was so much greater. No wonder Lila didn't want to tell him. No wonder Lucas pushed for her to move here and for Charlie to protect her while he was on deployment.

"I'm sorry I made you tell me this, but I'm glad I know. Now, I can make sure someone's with you at all times. In fact"—he started pacing again—"maybe I should put a tracker on you or something?"

Lila's mouth curved up a bit. "You're not putting a tracker on me."

Charlie wanted to say that they had to do something, the psycho could try this again, but he didn't want to scare her. "What does Lucas think?"

She looked at him. "It's Lucas. What do you think he said?"

"Right."

"Look, I know this is a lot to take. But it happened six months ago. I'm in a much better place now, and nothing has happened since. Well, nothing big."

Charlie took a step back so he could see her better. "What do you mean 'nothing big'?"

She glanced away. "Just a few random emails, messages on Facebook, a Charlotte paper delivered to my apartment today that I didn't order. That kind of thing. None of them were from him or anything, but they were weird. Probably just weirdos messing around."

"But maybe not. You should have told me."

"So you could what?"

He didn't freaking know, but something had to be done. "Look, he might own the cops in Charlotte, but you know as well as I do that in Crestler's Key we look out for our own. They won't put up with this shit here, even if he is rich and has a fancy lawyer. Regardless, you're staying with me until we can be sure you're safe." Lila opened her mouth to argue, but he waved her off. "Nah, ah, Tiny Girl, you are with me every waking moment until we get this under control."

"Charlie. It's fine, really. This happened a long time ago. And I have to work. I can't stay attached to your hip."

Charlie wracked his brain for what to do, because she was right— she had to work, to live. He couldn't imprison her at his place and watch her every moment of every day. "Fine. You can work and then I'll pick you up. Take you there, too." He paced again, trying to work through it all. "I still think the tracker thing is a good idea. I know a guy who—"

She stood up then and walked toward him, then she wrapped her arms around his neck, comforting him, and he nearly lost it right there.

"I'm fine."

He gently stroked her hair. "I know you are. But no one should have to go through life afraid. Let me take away the fear. Let me help you."

"You already have."

Charlie's gaze met hers, before dropping to her lips. She was so close and his emotions were out of control, his care for her taking over all logical thought. "I won't let anything happen to you."

"Because I'm your friend or because . . . ?"

"Because one lazy day out on a hammock, I handed you my heart, and I don't think I ever got it back." And with those words went the last of his control, his need to have her close to him greater than his need to appease his friend.

His mouth came down on hers, and suddenly, he no longer cared about anything, not Lucas, not himself, only this moment. A surge of emotions hit him all at once—confusion and happiness, guilt and relief, each more conflicted than the last, but one thing was 100 percent clear—she was kissing him back. And that single thing meant there was no turning back. If she wanted him, he was there.

He wrapped his arms around her waist, securing her to him, as he deepened the kiss, ten years' worth of pent-up emotions and desires pouring out of him, all the things he wanted to say and couldn't, all the times he wanted to tell her and turned away instead. But now she was here, and Lucas wasn't, and she needed him to be more than a friend. She needed him to show her in a way that only going past friendship could show that she was safe and cared for, that his very existence was focused on looking out for her, to step in front of her and shield her from danger. Lucas might be a world away, but Charlie was here, and he refused to let her go.

She pressed her body against his, clearly eager for more, and the kiss deepened. His tongue slid over her mouth, begging her to let him inside. She opened, allowing him in, and he went to work, teasing and sampling, absorbed in her taste and feel. And when she gripped his back and moaned lightly into his mouth, he lost his mind.

The fire had died out now, darkness finding them, the lanterns providing the only light. Everything about the moment intense and romantic. He scooped her into his arms and started for the tent, his wants trumping any doubts, and laid her down on his sleeping bag, then stared down at her, so damn beautiful it hurt.

"I want you. I want you so badly right now, I'm losing my mind here. But . . ."

"But . . ." she repeated, and he could see the hurt flash across her face.

"No, not that kind of *but*." Her gaze lifted, and he pressed on. "You just detailed the most horrible thing that's ever happened to you. The kind of thing that should never happen to anyone. Our emotions are high right now, and I don't want you making a mistake."

"I'm not."

A smile played at his lips. "All right, then. *I* don't want to make a mistake."

"This would be a mistake?"

"No. Never." He ran his hands through his hair and released a slow breath. "I'm trying to do the right thing here, and I gotta tell you, you're not making it easy to be good."

"Should I make it harder?"

He choked on a laugh. "Damn, where was this woman ten years ago? I'd have ditched Lucas in a heartbeat."

She smiled. "You wouldn't have, though."

"No . . . I wouldn't have." He stared down at her again, wishing this was easier. Wishing Lucas understood that, with Lila, it wasn't about attraction or quick sex. It was so much more. Maybe he could explain to him, help him see that he had real feelings for her. "I need to talk to him first."

"I can't have you asking my brother for permission to be with me."

Charlie laughed again. "Who do you think I am? I'm not asking anybody for permission for anything. This is about us. I just want to handle it the right way. And the right thing to do is to tell him before we take it further. Let him react, and then you can make sure this is what you want. Because if it is, if I'm who you want to be with, then I am there. Yours."

"You're mine," she said in a small voice, like she was processing the words.

"I've been yours for a very long time."

He crawled beside her. "And if it's okay, I'd like to sleep here, beside you. So long as you can promise to be a good girl. Not sure I can resist you twice."

She grinned. "Okay."

They snuggled up together, and without bothering to change, they fell asleep wrapped in each other's arms. And for the first time in a long time, Charlie thought that future he'd envisioned all those years ago, Lila forever by his side, might finally become a reality.

Chapter Fourteen

The next day, Lila and Charlie hit up another trail with a new purpose—to try to catch some rainbow trout. Lots of trout, hopefully, but Lila had her doubts about her catching anything other than water.

While Lila had been fishing with her family before, she had never fished rivers or streams. Her idea of fishing was in a boat on the lake, the sun above, while she cast, reeled, and cast again, never getting the first bite, while her expert-angler brother caught fish after fish. Eventually, she'd get tired of his gloating and would ditch the pole in favor of a good book.

So when Charlie mentioned they'd be fishing a mountain stream, from the shore because he hadn't brought waders or the gear for fly-fishing, she thought maybe he'd be fishing. She would be lucky if she threw the lure into the right spot to even tempt a fish, let alone catch one.

To Charlie's credit, he hadn't mentioned her attack, likely in an effort to keep her distracted, but occasionally she would find him looking around, searching for something, then he'd glance at her and take her hand, gripping it tightly, before continuing on.

She wanted to assure him that everything was fine, no way could Wyatt be here. Besides, after she listened to her lawyer's voicemail from yesterday, she got the impression that someone within the police department felt Wyatt could be responsible for the disappearances and was keeping a sharp eye on his every move.

She was fine.

They were fine.

But just the same, she glanced down at the pistol protruding from Charlie's waistband, tucked inside his shirt, out of view and yet clearly there. Never in her life had she felt a gun was necessary to feel protected. Her family owned them for hunting and such, and of course, Lucas had them, but never had she considered buying one for herself. And never would she have thought she would feel so relieved for one to be near her. But then her assault changed her opinion on a lot of things.

"We're here," Charlie said, motioning to a stream ahead.

And wow. Forget fishing, Lila would be content to sit and take in the view. Clear, bubbling water glided over rocks, some large, some smaller. Pebbles cradled the edges, followed by green trees and foliage, the only sounds coming from the water as its current continued its path down the mountain.

"It widens just down there," Charlie said, pointing to their right. "Until it meets the falls. We'll scour the shore for slower moving pools, then fish upstream. Rainbows tend to like to hide, and they have amazing sight, so we have to be careful not to cast a shadow on the water, or we'll spook them."

"That's a lot to think about."

He grinned. "It is, but you get in a rhythm. And just wait until you hook one. They're strong, will fight you hard to get off. You'll need to show them your muscle if you hope to reel one in."

She pointed at herself. "Wait, me? No, no. I'm like an anti-fisherman or something. I've never caught a fish, despite all the trips I've been on with my family. They catch them, even my mom. But me? Yeah, I repel them."

Charlie's smile spread. "Maybe you never had the right teacher."

"Ah," Lila said, smiling too now. "So you're going to show me the path to fishing greatness? Teach me the real way to do it? Like a fishing Yoda."

He laughed. "Yeah, I don't know about a Yoda, but I've never been up here and left without a fish. Besides, if you don't catch one, what are we going to eat tonight? This is survival, baby. We either hook 'em or go hungry. Kind of elevates the game. You up for the challenge?" The glint in his eyes stirred something in her belly, and despite the joking nature of the conversation, she found herself leaning in closer, pressing her lips easily to his. A surprised expression crossed his face.

"Sorry, I couldn't resist."

"Please . . . feel free to lose your self-control anytime."

Now it was Lila's turn to laugh, the feeling spreading out in her chest, making her forget for a moment that she'd been in a dark place just months ago, unable to get out of bed, to eat, to sleep. "I like this. You make things easy, better."

"I just told you that you have to catch a fish to eat and you call that easy? Man, I need to work on my poker face. But I'll take it, if it gets me more of your attention." His gaze dropped to her mouth, and he pecked her lips lightly, then again, this time a second longer, before he groaned and pulled back. "Damn Lucas," he muttered, before nodding to the stream and taking a deliberate step away from her.

"Let's start up there. I've had good luck with that bend." He pointed with one of the poles he had carried, and then he started away, and Lila thought about the change happening between them. What would Charlie do if Lucas said no, he wasn't okay with this? Would Charlie walk away from her? Would he choose his friendship with Lucas over what they could share together? She wouldn't blame him and would respect him for honoring their friendship. She loved Lucas, and she would never want him to be uncomfortable, but at what point did her opinion on all of this begin to matter?

She was still lost in her thoughts when they stopped on the shore by a small, open area of water with a large rock sticking out from its depths. Charlie set down his tackle box and passed her a rod, then opened the tackle box, took out something that looked an awful lot like Play Doh, and put the hook through it.

"What is that?"

"It's called PowerBait, and trout love the stuff. Especially rainbows. But their appetite can change quickly, so I have a few other things up my sleeve. And if we get really desperate, I brought some soft cheese and corn."

Lila laughed. "Wow, are you going to offer them some steak, too?"

"You laugh now, but just wait."

He prepped his rod, then directed her over to the stream's edge. The sun peeked through the trees here and there, creating a kaleidoscope effect on the water. The air smelled like fresh rain, though the sky was clear, hardly a cloud in sight. And despite the fact that they were halfway up a mountain, Lila with no clue how to get back down without Charlie's assistance, she wasn't worried. Or nervous. Or scared.

She was happy.

"All right, Mr. Pro Angler, show me how it's done."

Charlie cast into the water, inside the bend and just beside the rock. He reeled slowly, slowly, then all of a sudden he jerked his rod up. "Got 'em." He started reeling, then sighed. "Damn, he got off."

Lila set down her own rod and cracked her knuckles dramatically, then shook out her shoulders. "Maybe you should let me show you how it's done."

Beaming, Charlie took a step back. "By all means, Tiny. Show me how a real pro does it."

It was all for fun, and Lila knew she stood about as much chance of catching a fish as she did of getting struck by lightning in that moment. But it was fun to pretend, and she'd be lying if she said she didn't enjoy having Charlie's eyes on her.

She followed the basic knowledge she had of fishing and combined it with what she'd seen Charlie do, then cast out to the same rock Charlie had fished moments before.

And everything went just fine for about ten seconds. Fine and altogether innocent. She held the rod and reeled every once in a while and smirked arrogantly over at Charlie, with his cute cargo shorts and Southern Dive T-shirt and backwards baseball cap. But then her smirking turning to looking, which turned to straight checking him out and how perfectly his T-shirt covered his thick biceps, and then she remembered that first day she'd seen him at the animal hospital, no shirt, all those defined muscles visible for her to drool over. Only she hadn't checked them out, not nearly enough anyway. And now she found herself wishing that she could ask him to take the shirt off, it was a hot day after all, so she could—

"Whoa!" Something yanked on her rod, and she fumbled with it, nearly dropping it to the ground as she tried to remember what to do and how to do it.

"You got one!" Charlie called.

Panic raced through her. "Me? But I don't know what to do!"

"Set the hook, reel him in, don't let him off."

What and what and what? Which was she supposed to do first and how? She gripped the pole and started reeling, but holy hell this fish was fighting. Suddenly heat roared to life inside her and sweat tricked down her back that had nothing to do with the smoking hot man beside her and everything to do with this damn fish and his epic determination to get off her hook. But oh no, this was the first fish she'd ever caught—accident or not—and by God he was not getting away.

"All right, steady the rod so it's secure and wear him out. Let him take the line out a little, then reel him in. You don't want to reel too fast or he'll snap the line and get away."

Lila tried to follow Charlie's instructions, to steady the rod, but the little joker was pulling hard, and she felt her own biceps coming to life to try to keep the pole from flying into the water, the fish taking it away like a souvenir. "How do I get him over here? He's beating the crap out of me."

Charlie started to laugh, until Lila glared over at him, and he covered it up with a cough. "Okay, rest the end of your rod here," Charlie said, adjusting it so it rested against her hip. "There, now choke up on the rod, closer to the reel. Good," he said, his hand covering hers, and then his chest was against her back, and she drew in that lemony-spice scent of his, and almost dropped the damn pole again. He chuckled against her ear. "Easy, Tiny Girl. Remember we need that fish for dinner."

"Then you should probably take a step back, because I'm seconds away from saying screw the fish and attacking you."

He went still, and Lila worried that she'd said too much too soon, but before she could worry too much about it, the trout splashed above water. "You got him now. Reel!"

And she did, slowly, then harder, then slow again, until Charlie had the net ready and grabbed him with the net. "Woohoo!" He took the fish out of it and then held it out toward her, his thumb in the fish's mouth, holding it tight.

"Grab him. We gotta get a pic of your first catch. Then you can clean it."

"Are you insane? I don't know how to clean a fish."

He handed the fish to her, and she lifted it up, smiled as he snapped several pictures with his iPhone, then he took the fish from her and placed it in the small cooler he'd brought with them. "But you're a vet."

She nodded slowly. "Exactly. My job is to keep animals alive, not learn all the ways to properly kill and cook them."

"Ah, good point. All right, I'll clean it, while you cook the veggies. Deal?"

"You giving up on catching one so soon?"

With one look, he grabbed his rod and set off back to the river's edge. "See, I was going to let you have your win and celebrate, but oh no, you have to throw a man's dignity on the line. So no, I'm not giving up. We'll keep this little game going and make a little wager of it. Go by weight. Whoever weighs in the most fish, wins."

Lila placed her hands on her hips and narrowed her eyes at him. "And what does the winner get?"

Charlie's attention drifted to the water as he considered what the fishing champion would win. "How about a massage?"

She cocked an eyebrow. "A massage? As in your hands on me, or my hands on you?"

"Bad idea?"

A mischievous smile took over her face. "I can handle it if you can," she said, a challenge in her tone.

"Oh, I can handle."

Lila grabbed her rod and went back to her place. "We shall see, Mr. Fisherman. We shall see."

"So, that's what your sore-loser face looks like?" Charlie asked with a grin as he peered over at Lila. "*Hm*, interesting. I gotta say I kind of like it."

They had fished for another hour and ended up catching the same number of fish, but Charlie's fish had outweighed Lila's by a pound, so he became the winner, bragging rights and all. The only problem was the prize—the massage.

Because, while he'd told Lila he could handle it, now that said massage was before them, he wasn't so sure. Charlie liked to think of himself as an honorable man, but he was also human, hormones and all, and he couldn't guarantee his thoughts wouldn't drift into dishonorable territory if Lila put her hands on him. And if she straddled his waist while giving the massage, then all bets were off. He wasn't a superhero, after all. He was a man, and there wasn't a man alive that could resist a woman like Lila if things became intimate. Which meant he needed to avoid the massage at all costs.

"Deep thought?" Lila asked as she went to work preparing the corn on the cob.

Charlie watched her with interest. "You cook it unshucked?"

Lila glanced up from her work. "Of course."

Charlie scratched his head, not fully convinced. "You sure?"

"Want another bet? I'll grill yours shucked and mine unshucked. You can taste each. If the unshucked is better, you owe me a movie night, popcorn and all. If the shucked is better, then you choose the date. But you have to be honest."

"Date?"

Suddenly, her eyes went back to the corn, and he watched her remove the outer leaves from one, wrap it in foil and then twist the ends to secure it. "You know, just a friend date."

"Right, like this." Only nothing about this met the description for *friend*, and if they went through with the massage, then any hopes of friendship would be out the window—or tent, in this case.

"Exactly. So, you agree?"

Charlie stared at her, wishing he could say no, that they needed to take a step back. Something, anything. But instead his mouth refused to listen to his brain and he heard himself saying, "Deal."

"But you have to be honest."

"I'll always be honest with you."

He noticed her throat working as she attempted to swallow, and he wanted to ask if this was okay, whatever they were doing—being this close to each other. But how could he ask without starting a conversation he wasn't prepared to have?

Instead, he released a breath and went back to seasoning the trout while she shucked his ear of corn, her focus fully on the task before her, though he could tell she was bothered by something. Guilt punched him in the gut. How long could he continue being loyal to Lucas while hurting Lila?

The fish went on the grill, and they sat back in their chairs, watching the fire, neither of them speaking, the silence painful. And he couldn't take it anymore.

"I'm sorry."

She pulled her legs into the chair, her arms wrapped around them again. It was a move she'd mastered as a kid, one she pulled out whenever she was uncomfortable. He didn't want her to feel uncomfortable around him. "There's nothing for you to be sorry for."

He laughed sarcastically. "Are you kidding? There's a lot I need to be sorry for. Every day is a tug-of-war over which person I risk hurting, and I hate it. It's not what I want or who I want to be. I only really care about a handful of people, and right now I'm messing up. I just don't know how to fix it."

"Can I ask you something and you'll be honest with me?" Lila asked.

"Of course."

The fire crackled as it worked through the wood and twigs Charlie had pulled together when he built it. The smells of the food cooking floated all around them. Night hovered above, while the stream continued its melody in the distance. It was a perfect evening, and yet as he waited for Lila's question, nothing in him felt at peace. His thoughts were everywhere, his heart picking up speed, his hands restless with the desire to do something. If he couldn't fix their situation, surely he could fix something.

"What do you want?" she asked, her voice even despite the tension on her face.

He looked over at her. "I think I made that clear last night."

"Did you? Because it feels like we take one step forward and five back. I feel you there, sense you looking at me, but then you pull away. You said if I wanted you then you were mine. Well, I do. I want you. I want this."

Without thinking, he reached out and took her hand. "I don't know what to say. I feel like I've started this, but Lucas's out there, and the right thing to do is to tell him first. It just is. He specifically asked me not to do what I'm doing. How can I go there against his wishes? How can I take this to the next level without at least respecting him enough to tell him first? Because he's going to be livid, freak out. He's going to shout and scream, but at least if I haven't already crossed the line, then we can talk about it. Help him see that this, you and me, could be great. But if I've already betrayed his trust, I can't get it back. Do you understand?"

Lila stared at the fire again. "I do . . . but I think we crossed the line a long time ago."

The words hit Charlie dead on, and though he knew what she said was true, he didn't want to hear it. He'd tried to rationalize the whole thing in his head. A kiss wasn't sex. They hadn't professed any major feelings. They hadn't announced their engagement.

They'd kissed a few times, no big deal. Only that was a lie. It was a huge deal, and—damn it.

"How about we try not to worry about this yet? We'll tell Lucas as soon as he's home safe. Until then, it's fine."

But even though he heard the logic in her words, he could tell that this was hurting her. The uncertainty of it, the risk with no guarantee of reward. He was such a jackass.

"Now stop staring at me with that guilt-stricken face. You're hotter when you smile." She flashed her trademark grin in his direction, and he couldn't help but offer his own back.

"Let's eat. An empty stomach won't fix a thing."

They worked together to get plates and bottled water for each of them, divvied out the trout, and then Lila brought over the corn. "All right, here you go, Mr. Know-It-All. The taste test. Here's yours," she said, dropping an ear of corn on his plate. "And here's mine." She did the same with her own, then focused back on him. "You get the first bite."

"All right, but don't get your hopes up. I've been grilling corn the same way for a long time." He took a bite of his corn, let the sweetness coat his taste buds. Damn, he'd forgotten how much he loved grilled corn. He was tempted to take a second bite, his stomach groaning at him to hurry up and feed it, but he promised Lila he'd give her corn a real shot. Still, he didn't think it could top what he'd just tried. Until he took a bite of hers and juicy sweetness exploded in his mouth. The unshucked corn was twice as juicy and flavorful, all the deliciousness of the first corn but multiplied.

"So?" Lila asked, obvious nervousness in her voice.

"So, I'm taking this one." He tried to walk off with her corn and she took off after him, jumping to try to grab it as he held it high in the air, out of her reach. "Fine, just one more bite."

"Fine."

But as he lowered the corn, she snatched it from his grasp and took off, both of them laughing now. And Charlie knew, even if Lucas said no, even if he said he'd never speak to him again, Charlie couldn't turn away. He was in too deep now. Lila was right—they had already crossed the line.

There was no going back.

Chapter Fifteen

A light rain started during dinner, so they quickly packed everything up and by the time they dashed into the tent, they were both soaked through, their clothes suctioned to their skin, hair dripping.

Lila rung out her tank top and then pushed her hair out of her face. "Got any towels?" she asked, laughing, but nothing was humorous about the look on Charlie's face.

His eyes had drifted down, where they stayed, and Lila realized that her white tank top, so very innocent moments before, now revealed every outline of her lace bralette, and because it, too, was white, you could now plainly see the outline of her nipples.

"We need to change," Lila said, clearing her throat. "Then we can finalize this bet. Fair warning, I'm kind of amazing."

"Yeah . . ." But Charlie made no effort to move, and instead, his gaze returned to meet her own, and he shook his head slowly. "You are amazing. And smart. And kind. And beautiful. So damn beautiful, and you don't even realize it. You don't see what the world sees. What I see. And I can't freaking pull myself away. Can't even be around you without wanting to touch you. So you can forget the bet. I'll forfeit now. Because if you touch me, if you put your hands on my body, I'm not sure I'll be able to stop this from going further. Hell, you're not even touching me right now and it's taking everything in me to stay over here."

Lila contemplated what he was saying, tried to make sense of his fear over losing Lucas. But she knew her brother. Sure, he might be mad, but he loved Charlie and he loved Lila. It would all be okay.

So with that in mind, she took a step toward him, her eyes on his, forcing him to look at her. "No."

"No?" His eyebrows rose.

"No, a bet is a bet. Now lie down."

He licked his teeth as if in thought, and holy hell, it had to be the sexiest thing Lila had ever seen in her life. Her body buzzed with the need to touch him, to feel his warm skin under her fingertips. "You want me to lie down." He said it as a statement, not a question, but she could see the apprehension on his face. How hard he was fighting the tension building in the air. Rain beat against the tent, the storm rolling in, and with it Lila found courage she'd never felt before. There was no one else here, only them. No one around to judge, no one to remind them that she was Lila and he was Charlie. Just them.

"Lie down."

He eyed her once more, and then slowly started for his sleeping bag, when Lila called out, stopping him. "Shirt off first."

Now he was staring at her, doubt on his face. "Lila . . ."

"No shirt. I can't massage you with a shirt on. That'll never work. I'll be a good girl."

"Is that a promise?"

Hell, no. "Yes."

Charlie's eyes met hers, heat within them as he gripped the edge of his shirt and slipped it off, dropping it without thought to the ground. And before Lila could stop herself, her own eyes trailed over his chest. The small dive-flag tattoo on his left pectoral muscle, the cut of each of his abdominal muscles, the deep *V* that disappeared below his low-hanging shorts.

"Ready now?" he asked, his voice low and husky, laced with want.

Lila tried to swallow, but she couldn't make her throat work. "Good. Lie down."

Without another word, Charlie lowered himself to his knees, and then his arm and back muscles flexed as he dropped down to his stomach.

Now or never, Lila thought. She took off her tank top and dropped it with Charlie's shirt, and then walked over and stepped over him, one leg on each side of him, then she bent down until she straddled his ass, his smooth back laid out before her.

She glided her hands over his body until she reached his shoulders, and a shiver worked through him, a curse slipping from his lips, as he clenched his eyes closed.

Slowly, she worked her hands into his hot muscles, pressing and massaging, working out the tension she felt in his shoulder muscles. Then she leaned over him more and went to his neck, working those muscles, until he moaned low, and she smiled with pleasure.

"This okay?"

"This is killing me."

Lila bit her lip and worked her way down his back, pressing harder, deeper in spots, lighter in others, then started back up, heat building in her belly, then lower, swirling and igniting, until she knew she must be soaked. Her hands went over his biceps, and without realizing it, she rocked against him, desperate for relief. Instantly, his eyes flew open. "Screw it." And then he flipped around, causing her to gasp. His pupils darkened as he drank her in, and then he pulled her against him, his mouth covering hers, his tongue commanding her to follow along. To not stop. He gripped her ass and tugged her closer, and then as quickly as he'd flipped around earlier, he flipped them over so she rested on the ground now, him over her, his lips on her neck, her collarbone, sucking and tasting, and then as though he'd lost all sense of control, he pressed a hot kiss to her nipple through the lace bralette, and she arched back, moaning loudly as she gripped his head. "Again," she breathed.

He sucked her deep into his mouth, lace and all, tonguing the sensitive flesh, as his free hand snaked down to cup her heat. His hand slipped into her shorts, then inside her panties, stroking her core.

"So wet," he said, his words as breathless as her own. Then he slipped two fingers inside her, gentle at first and then harder, faster, finding a rhythm, until she couldn't think, couldn't process, only feel. Before she could stop herself, she exploded, stars flashing across her vision, her body firing in sparks and spasms as she came around his fingers.

Lila drew a few breaths to calm herself down, and then reached down, his need visible through his shorts. She stroked him once through the shorts and he groaned, then took her hand and gingerly placed it down at her side, then curled up on her other side and pulled her against him.

"You have to let me—"

"This wasn't about me. It was about you, your need."

"But—"

"*Shhh*, I'm trying to sleep," he said as he nuzzled closer to her.

"Yeah, but—"

"*Shhh*, sleep."

Lila wracked her brain for how to respond, a way to convince him, but she could tell that he wasn't bending on this, and suddenly all the feelings she'd had for him before multiplied, overwhelming her. This wasn't just selfless, it was caring and kind. Because she did need this, to her core she needed this. For him to realize that, for him to put her first was so—

"Are you crying?"

She sniffled. "No."

Charlie jerked upright, his eyebrows knitted together. "Did I—?"

"No, I just . . . I don't know, okay? I'm a woman. We do this sometimes."

Charlie chuckled as he pulled her against him again. "You go ahead and cry, Tiny. But just be prepared. The real thing? Yeah, it might throw you into a full-out depression." He paused, and then, "That didn't come out right, did it?"

They burst out laughing, and though Lila didn't know where this thing of theirs was going, she knew she would never forget that night.

Chapter Sixteen

An hour had passed since Charlie kissed Lila goodbye, and he still couldn't stop smiling.

They slept wrapped in each other's arms all night, and then a call from the farm—that Zac was needed and Charlie would need to come back early to cover the shop—forced them to leave the mountains earlier than planned. Truthfully, he could have stayed there forever, the rest of the world forgotten, just the two of them and nature.

Once back in Crestler's Key, Lila went on to the farm to check the animals, and Charlie went to Southern Dive, and though he'd seen her an hour before, he already missed her. The thought made his smile widen. It had been a long time since he had cared enough about a woman to miss her.

He had just opened his laptop to check online orders so he could pull, package, and ready them for the afternoon FedEx pickup, when his cell rang. There was no one in the shop yet, most of the rush happening in the early afternoon, so he contemplated letting it go to voicemail so he could get in the orders before the shop became busy. But then he thought of Lila, and his heart did that weird flip thing it'd been doing since their night together, and he grabbed the phone, far too eager, but it wasn't Lila's name shining back at him. It was Lucas.

With trepidation, he answered the call, his nerves coiling tight. Lucas rarely called him when he was on deployment, so for him to call now something had to be wrong. "Hey, man. You all right?" he asked.

"Yeah, good. Just checking in." There was a lot of noise in the background, and Charlie wanted to ask where he was, but he knew Lucas couldn't say.

"You staying safe?"

"You know nobody out here's got anything on me." The men laughed, but there was nothing about it that was funny. Lucas continuously risked his life, but talking about that fact didn't change it, so it was easier for them both to make light of it.

"Actually, I was going to ask you how you thought Lila was doing? I talked to her a bit ago and she seemed . . . distracted."

Shit.

Charlie opened his mouth to tell him everything, but closed it back up immediately. He couldn't tell him when he was out there, always in danger, when this information could cause him stress and in turn put his life at risk. No, they needed to wait until Lucas was back. "I think she's okay. She told me about what happened to her. It was hard for her to talk about it, but she seemed better after."

"Damn, I wish I were there."

"I know you do. But I've got her. We're planning to hit the shooting range later this week, and then she's staying active with work at the hospital and then at my farm. She's strong."

"Yeah, yeah she is," Lucas said. Then someone said something to him on his end, and he quickly said he had to run and would call back when he could.

"Take care of yourself, all right?" Charlie said.

"You too. And Lila. I appreciate everything you're doing for her. Not sure what I'd do without you."

They said good-bye, and Charlie set down his phone, a knot in his stomach that hadn't been there moments before. This guilt was going to eat him alive, but what could he do?

Nothing. He wouldn't push Lila away. Not again.

Lila walked into Crestler's Key Animal Hospital with pep in her step, her smile stretching from ear to ear, and it wasn't going anywhere anytime soon.

It was the first time that she had opened up about the accident and felt better after, not worse. Having Charlie there, his arms wrapped around her, made her feel strong. Like maybe she wasn't just a victim. She was a survivor, strong and able. He'd helped her see that, and then last night had been . . . wow. She was still reeling, her excitement in seeing him later almost too much to stand.

"Hey there, Dr. Jacobs, you look happy," Tracy said from the front desk. Today she was dressed in a light blue T-shirt with a cartoon dog on it and a skirt, bright red-rimmed glasses completing her look. Tracy had lost her husband a few years ago to a sudden heart attack, and as far as Lila had heard, she hadn't dated since. But she was adorable and so nice. Maybe Lila should add her to her goals list, along with Annie. And then something occurred to her—she was happy, like her friend in Charlotte, and in turn wanted everyone around her to be happy. The bubbly feeling that took over was happening to her, maybe for the first time in her life.

"I am happy. How about you?" she asked, nearly bouncing, but then the older woman started in on a tirade of her aching back and an ingrown toenail, and suddenly Lila wished she'd kept it to a hello and nothing more. Perhaps Tracy could handle her own love life after all.

"I'm sorry to say, honey, that you might not be happy for long. Baxter asked for you to help in grooming."

Her eyes went wide. "Grooming?"

"They're short-handed in there today, and the place is already packed. I can't leave here, and there's no one else to help. Well, no one except Baxter, but you know how that goes." She rolled her eyes just as the phone rang, and she lifted her index finger to signal for Lila to wait while she answered the call.

Lila took the opportunity to peer around the animal hospital. Sure enough it was empty, every seat in the waiting area empty. And then she glanced through the glass door that led to the grooming area, and sure enough, chaos ensued, dogs barking loudly from their crates where they waited, and Jenny, the groomer, was covered in suds. She wiped her sleeve across her forehead, causing more suds to attach to her hair, and Lila's heart went out to her.

When she was getting her undergraduate degree, she'd helped out a groomer, so maybe that was why Baxter thought of her. And not at all because she was a woman and he was a man and clearly it would be her job to do anything that resembled cleaning, including the dogs. Because that was sexist, and surely he wouldn't pull such an obvious sexist stunt. But then this was Baxter.

Tracy hung up and then walked around to Lila where she still stood, staring at the grooming fiasco.

"Want me to get you an apron?" Tracy cocked her head to the side as an especially large dog jumped away from Jenny and took off around the room. "Or a rain jacket?"

Lila sighed. "Not sure anything will help that craziness, but thanks. I'll get on in there. Let me know if anyone shows, though, and I'm needed out here. Where is Baxter, anyway?"

"Oh, you know. Golfing. Or about to be. He's probably still outside."

"Golfing?"

The office manager's face switched to anger. "Yep, every Sunday. He plays, we work. That's a man for you."

And Lila had heard enough. Not all men were like Baxter, and while she wanted to explain this to Tracy, right now she needed to get outside and give her boss a piece of her mind.

"Be right back," she said to Tracy. Then she pivoted on her heels and marched out the front door, down the steps of the front porch and marched around to the back of the building, where sure enough, Baxter was placing a large black golf bag into the back of his SUV.

"Dr. Baxter, may I have a word?" Lila asked, fighting to keep her voice even. Her hands were shaking. She rarely got this upset, and every time she did, her hands would shake like a leaf, but enough was enough.

The old man sighed heavily and turned around to look at her. "What is it, Lila?"

"Dr. Jacobs."

"That's what I said, dear. Now, I have a tee time to get to."

Lila gritted her teeth together and flashed a good ole Southern smile, lest she chew his head off. "Actually, you didn't. You called me *Lila* and then *dear*. But I'm a doctor, just like you, and I would appreciate you referring to me as such when I am here. And furthermore, this"—she said, pointing to his golf bag—"is ridiculous. You have assigned me to grooming while you go golfing? I don't think so. I am a veterinarian, and my job is to provide care to animals. Not clean up their vomit. Not bathe them. I am happy to be a team player, I love being a team player, but I will not be treated like this anymore. So either you give me clients and their animals to care for, or I quit. Effective immediately."

He stared at her, not blinking, not making a face. Just staring. The sky was astonishingly blue, the sun too bright, and Lila wished she had sunglasses on so she could better read his reaction. As it were, with the sun's glare blinding her, she could scarcely see a few inches in front of her face.

He huffed. "All right, fine. You don't have to get so testy. I'll split the business with you beginning on Monday. Okay? Go on home. It's a Sunday, and we've got nothing going on today. If Tracy needs you, she'll call you. I'll let Jenny know to call in her daughters to help with the grooming. They love that." He smiled, and Lila tried to make sense of what all he'd just said.

It was the nicest thing she'd ever heard him say and the only time she'd ever seen him smile. Probably the only time he ever had in his life. For a second she contemplated telling him he should do it more often, smiling was a good look on him, but then the frown returned.

"Well, what are you staring at? Head on home before I change my mind."

"Right! I'm gone." Lila took off for her car, giggling like crazy the moment she stepped inside, and without consciously deciding to do it, she set off for Southern Dive.

The streets were quiet for a Saturday, and whereas normally Lila might struggle to find a spot to park around the dive shop, which was situated nicely at the end of Main Street, today she found one without a problem.

She pulled into an open spot, and immediately checked her face in the mirror for anything crazy, and then realizing what she'd just done, sat back in her seat. "Holy wow. I just checked my makeup. For a guy."

Lila searched her memory, and she could not remember the last time she'd worried about such a thing. Her focus had been on school, followed by her first job in Charlotte, and so personal care fell to the back of her list of concerns. After all, there was only so much time in the day. And it wasn't that she never checked her reflection in her car's mirror. It was more that she'd never done it out of nervousness over what a guy would think. At least not since she was in high school, a freshman, Charlie a senior, and yeah, she'd stared at the mirror for an hour every time Lucas announced he'd be coming over.

Charlie. Oh my God, she was going to see Charlie. Who, by all accounts, likely wanted to see her, too. She could hardly contain her excitement.

She'd just decided to stop being silly and get in there, when a knock on her window had her jerking back.

"Hey!" Audrey called, waving.

Pushing open her car door, Lila stepped out and hugged her friend. "Hey, there. What are you doing here?"

"Oh, you know, nothing really. And not at all hoping to run into Brady while doing that nothing."

Lila's eyebrows went up. "Wait a second. Did you two . . . ?"

Audrey bit her lip. "No, well . . . maybe. Do you remember that night we were all at Maguire's? You left with Charlie early? I offered to drive Brady home since we live in the same area, and this led to that and . . . well, I might have slept at his place that night." She winked.

"You so did not go home with Brady Littleton!"

She chewed her lip again. "I so did. And now, I'm wondering if he's thinking about a do-over, because honestly, I can't stop thinking about him. Which is stupid. But there it is. Anyway, it's just my luck that I'd run into you here. Now you can be my cover."

"Your cover?" Lila asked skeptically.

"Just follow my lead."

They stepped up to the main door, and Audrey opened and held it for Lila.

There were male voices coming from the right, but they went quiet as soon as the women were inside. Lila's gaze travelled over to where the voices had been and immediately locked on Charlie. He stared back at her, while a slow smile crept across her face. "Hey, you."

"Hey yourself," she said.

"No way. You didn't." This was from Brady, but Lila couldn't pull her eyes away from Charlie enough to see what his brother was talking about. "I knew you were going to go there. Zac, you owe me fifty bucks."

But Zac wasn't paying attention to Brady. He was staring at Charlie. "Can I talk to you for a second? Alone."

"No."

"Dude," Zac said, his tone harder this time.

"Not now." Then Charlie walked out from behind the small counter and started for her. Each step sent her heart racing, butterflies dancing through her belly, her insides coming alive.

He stopped a few inches away from her and her body buzzed with the desire to touch him, kiss him. "I thought you were at work."

"I was. Good ole Bax let me go early."

He grinned. "So you came here?"

"I came here. I hope that's okay. I had some stuff to show you, but you look busy so we can go over it later if you'd like."

Charlie opened his mouth to reply, when Zac called to him again, and Lila wondered what was going on.

"Are we interrupting you?" She glanced from Charlie to Zac and then back.

"No. He's fine. Let's go outside."

Opening the door for her, Charlie waited until Lila was outside and the door was closed to speak again. "Everything okay?" he asked as they started down the sidewalk. Most of the shops sat dark, a typical Sunday in Crestler's Key.

"Yeah, I just wanted to show you a few things." She took out her cell, went to her Etsy app, and clicked on a few of the businesses she'd saved there that morning before she went into work. "Look, there's all kinds of T-shirt businesses that operate fully through Etsy. You could maybe start there to build up the business or even to check how well it's going to work before fully launching on your site."

Charlie took her phone and swiped through the T-shirts while Lila watched him. Maybe she'd chosen bad designs, but still, it would give him an idea of the possibilities. Finally, he handed her phone back with a smile. "You researched this for me?"

"I know these aren't as good as yours. They're just examples. But I know you can do this. It's a chance, sure, but I think it could be amazing."

"I think you're amazing." He took her hand and they fell into an easy silence as they walked, when Lila glanced back at Southern Dive, her curiosity taking over.

"What was that about back there?"

"What do you mean?"

"Zac. He seemed . . . I don't know. Upset, maybe?" Lila thought back to all the times she'd been around Zac and never once had he behaved so strangely toward her.

Charlie blew out a long, slow breath. "He wants me to talk to Lucas about us, and he's right. I want to talk to Lucas, too. But Lucas called me today, and I thought about telling him, and then I remembered where he is and what he's doing. This could seriously jack up his focus. I couldn't live with myself if something happened to him."

"No, you're right. We shouldn't say anything to him until he's back here."

"Right, so when he goes ballistic at least we'll know he's in a safe zone. Me, on the other hand? Yeah, no certainties there." Charlie laughed, but it didn't brighten his face like his real laugh would. Clearly, he was worried.

Lila thought about her brother, everything he'd done for her, and guilt hit in her chest. "I didn't realize he'd get so mad."

"You're his little sister."

"Not so little anymore."

His eyes sparked. "Noticed that."

She grinned. "How about dinner tonight? Or the movie, since you owe me a friend date."

"Dinner sounds great, but my place. I'll cook for you."

"You cooked for me last night."

He took a step closer to her and reached out for her other hand. "I'll cook for you every night if you'll let me."

Their gazes held and he inched in, but then commotion from inside Southern Dive had them glancing up the sidewalk to find Audrey storming out, Brady on her heels.

"*Uh-oh*," Charlie said.

"I better go check on her. See you tonight?"

Charlie released her hands and took a step backwards. "I'll be counting the minutes."

Chapter Seventeen

"Hey there, cutie, you had a package delivered," Annie called from her front porch. She was rocking in one of the white rockers situated on the porch and drinking a glass of tea. What a life. Lila thought for the first time in a long time that maybe she could have a life like that someday. Easy and lazy, just her, a rocker, a tall glass of sweet tea and a certain handsome man.

She sighed at the thought and waved to Annie. "Thank you, Ms. Annie!"

Lila had spent all afternoon talking to Audrey about Brady and what had happened. Apparently, she hoped they could go out, an official date and all, and Brady hoped they could keep things casual. In the end, it was probably for the best. Brady had a reputation for never settling down, never being content with a woman for more than a few weeks. Audrey deserved someone who would be there for her for the long haul.

Telling herself she'd send her friend a quick text to check in on her when she made it inside, she went up the steps where, sure enough, a large white envelope with her name on it but no return address rested against the door. *Hmm*, that was odd.

Opening the door, she kicked it back closed with her foot and examined the envelope closer. It was probably a telemarketer thing or something, but then she thought of her old friends, and how they had talked about coming to visit. She did give them her address, so maybe it was something from them.

She pulled out a knife from the silverware drawer and tore open the end of the envelope. Once opened, she emptied the contents onto the kitchen counter, only to feel all the blood drain from her body.

Before her lay a dozen or more four-by-six photos, all of her and

Charlie during their camping trip. Some were at the campsite, some were of them hiking. Others were of just close-ups of her face. And then one was of them kissing, his arms wrapped around her, their bodies pressed together, and suddenly Lila couldn't breathe.

Who would have done this? And then the answer hit her like a freight train, causing her legs to go weak and for her to slip to the floor. The knife clanged against the tile beside her.

"No, not again." She gripped her head as fear worked its way through her. "How could he find me?" Suddenly, it occurred to her that it wasn't safe here. She scanned the kitchen, the family room, and that was when she noticed the flowers on the table behind the couch, a dozen bright red roses staring back at her.

Slowly, she pushed herself to standing and walked over to the flowers. A tiny note stuck out from within their petals, and she took it, her hands shaking so badly she could hardly open it. Finally, she peered down at the words scribbled across the card.

Miss me?

A scream burst from her lips and she stumbled back, eyes searching everywhere. He had been there. Oh my God, he had been there, in her apartment. Could be there now, but no—it could have been Annie. Could be just a delivery to scare her, and Annie put them inside on the table.

She raced outside and down the steps, narrowly falling down them before she reached the bottom, not stopping until she stood before her landlord.

"Annie, did you put flowers on the table in there? Or maybe let a delivery person inside to set them down?"

Her brow quirked. "No, can't say I did. How nice, though, that you received flowers."

The last of the warmth in Lila's body disappeared, replaced by an icy cold. She turned slowly, eyeing the driveway, the trees. He could be anywhere. "Annie . . . do you have your phone?"

"Of course, honey, why?"

"Call 911."

Charlie finished slicing up all the peppers and onions for the faji-tas he planned to make Lila for dinner, hoping his memory served that they were a favorite. When they were younger, and Lila wasn't old enough for her license, Lucas and Charlie (because they always carpooled) drove her to school, and she used to beg them to take her to Taco Tuesday, the only Mexican restaurant in town, for their fajitas. She was addicted to them.

When he was living at the Keys, he stumbled across a favorite little Mexican joint that made the best fajitas he'd ever eaten in his life. He grew close to the owner and managed to get the recipe, Lila on his mind, but until now he'd never tried to make them.

With the veggies cut, he went to work mixing the spices he'd picked up, sure to eye the recipe as he went along. He'd just picked up the half-crumpled napkin with the recipe written on it to look over the next steps when a knock sounded from his front door, followed by another, then another, each more urgent than the last.

He dropped the recipe on the counter and wiped his hands on his jeans, setting off for the door, worry working through him. Lila was due in a half hour, but if she were early, then something must have happened. Or he could stop being paranoid and just open the door.

Pushing aside his worry, he opened the door to find Lila on the other side, an overnight bag in hand, her eyes wide with fear.

"What happened?"

She set her bag down and launched herself into his arms, her whole body shaking.

"Lila, girl, you gotta talk to me. I'm freaking out here. What happened? Is it Lucas? Is he . . . ?" He couldn't bring himself to finish that sentence, because it was impossible.

"No," she said, pulling back, then she spun around, her eyes searching outside, but for what he couldn't be sure. Charlie thought he might lose his mind.

"Seriously, I need to know what's happening here. You're scaring me."

"Maybe he followed me. No, but then. Oh my God." She clasped her hands together, and Charlie pulled her against him again.

"I've got you. Come inside. Tell me what happened." He closed the door and helped her to the couch, then stood over her, waiting.

"He found me," she said, terror-filled eyes meeting his.

"Wait—who?" Then realization worked through him. "No."

She nodded. "I went to my apartment and there was a package. An envelope. It had pictures, Charlie. Pictures of us." Lila's hands went out as though trying to grasp something and then coming up empty, she placed them in her lap again. "He had photos of us." The words were less for Charlie than for herself, and that fear there ignited something deep inside him.

"What photos?"

"From the camping trip. Hiking, at the campsite. K-kissing." She shook her head and ran her hands over her face.

"Freaking psycho. I will take him out myself."

"And then there were flowers inside my apartment. Annie said she didn't put them there, so it could only be him. He's here, Charlie."

Charlie took a step back, needing to process everything, his eyes on the window over his kitchen sink, visible from the family room due to the open floor plan, woods behind his backyard showing through the window. No one else lived around him. She was safe here . . . right? Suddenly he wasn't so sure.

"We need to call the cops."

"I did. They've been questioning me for the last hour. They took the photos and flowers, trying to find fingerprints or something. They're supposed to let me know, but otherwise there's nothing they can do right now. Nothing. I called my mom, and they want to come here or have me go there, but I don't want anyone else to be in danger. I don't know what to do." She put her head in her hands and he went to her, needing to make her feel protected, something.

"Look, you are safe here. I can promise you that. I'll call my brothers to let them know, have them spread the word. I'll call the station, too. We'll find this asshole. But in the meantime, gun laws in Kentucky are clear. I have a no-trespassing sign at the end of my driveway, and I'm legally in my right to shoot the bastard if he steps foot on my property." She nodded, but he could tell that she wasn't feeling better. Not yet, but he knew what would help. "Come with me."

"Where are we going?"

"Actually, hang here for a second. I'll be right back."

Charlie opened the basement door and went down the steps to his finished basement, then to his gun safe. He pressed his thumb to the fingerprint pad, and instantly the safe unlocked. Scanning his weapons, he chose a small 9mm pistol, checked that it was loaded, then went back upstairs.

Lila eyed the gun, then him, her eyebrows lifting.

"Target practice. Come on. I have one set up in the back. But you'll need these." He passed her a pair of shooting earmuffs, knowing she'd been around Lucas enough to know exactly what they were.

"I'm going to shoot it?"

"Yep. Right now if you're comfortable. I want you to be able to protect yourself. And this gun is lightweight enough that you should be able to handle it with ease."

They stepped outside, the sun long since hidden behind the trees, but there was still enough light to allow them to practice.

"Okay, you remember what Lucas taught you, right?"

She nodded, widening her stance, then Charlie handed her the gun. "Remember, muzzle control at all times. Know where you're pointing the gun; be aware."

"And this is a semiauto, not auto, right?" she asked, and Charlie couldn't help but grin.

"Darlin', your brother's the only one you know who can legally operate an automatic weapon, and that's only when he's on duty. And even then, he's likely using semiauto most of the time. NFA weapons like automatic firearms are restricted at the federal level by the National Firearms Act of 1934 and the Firearms Owners' Protection Act of 1986."

"You seem to know a lot about them," she said.

Charlie shrugged. "Owning a gun and carrying that gun is a serious thing. Too many idiots buy them and have no idea what they're doing. I make it a point to be well versed in gun laws for Kentucky and every neighboring state. And then, of course, I know the ins and outs of every weapon I own. That's just responsible gun ownership."

"So you have a lot, then?"

"No. But I have enough to take out this bastard if he decides he wants to gamble."

Each second she seemed to relax more, and Charlie felt pride in giving her this extra sense of protection. Lila had been around guns her whole life, and Lucas had taught her well. But this was the first time she was practicing for her own safety.

"Go ahead and put on your ear protection." She did as he asked, and then he walked her through how to shoot it. Charlie took a slight step back and motioned to the target several yards away from them. "Fire."

And she did, all her aggravation coming out in that one round.

She fired again and again, and Charlie sensed this was bringing her more relief than anything else he could have done.

Finally, she lowered the gun and peered over her shoulder at him. "How did I do?"

He eyed the target, several fresh bullet holes in it. "Damn, woman, I thought you said you haven't been to a shooting range in a while."

"I was taught by a professional, remember?"

"That you were."

Their eyes met, and he knew she was thinking about Lucas. "Would you feel safer if he were here?"

"No," she said, starting toward him. "I feel safe with you."

Charlie brushed her hair off of her face, then unable to hold back, pressed his lips easily to hers, the kiss a small assurance that he wouldn't let anything happen to her, but its impact on his body was immediate. Sparks and shocks like he'd never experienced coursed through him, settling in his gut, and he feared now that he'd opened himself up to the amazingness that was Lila, he might not ever be the same again.

"Hungry? I've got everything ready to cook."

"What are we having?"

He smiled. "Fajitas. I hope that's okay. You used to like them when we were younger."

"I can't believe you remembered that," she said smiling back. "They're my favorite."

Charlie took the gun from her, held the door open, then took her hand to stop her before she could go inside. "I like you being here, in my world."

"I like it, too."

They went back inside, and Charlie returned the gun to his safe. Then he cooked the chicken and threw in the spices and veggies, sautéing them while Lila made them both drinks.

"So you're a wine girl?"

She cocked her head, considering the question. "I like either. Depends on the mood."

"Tell me more," he called over his shoulder.

"Like what?"

"Everything. Tell me what adult Lila is like."

She sat down at one of the barstools across from where he was working. "Let's see. I love seafood, hate sushi."

He grinned. "Smart woman."

"I'm a dog person."

"Ah, Henry approves," he said, nodding to the dog fast asleep on his dog pillow.

"I hate that Lucas is in the army. I know that's terrible. I love him for it, I'm fiercely proud, but I miss him. We were always really close."

Nodding, Charlie finished up the fajitas and filled two plates with tortillas, meat, vegetables, and rice. "I miss him, too."

"And I like you."

Charlie's eyes lifted.

"A lot. I have liked you since I was eight years old and you and Lucas were ten and you let me tag along when you built that dam in the creek behind our house. Something about you stuck with me, and through all of it, even with both of us living far away, I never forgot you."

Tension sparked in the air as their gazes held, every fiber in Charlie's body begging him to go to her, but he feared if he went now, with their emotions high, he wouldn't be able to stop. And he had to stop. He had to think about Lucas.

"Now you tell me something," Lila said, saving him, and hell if he didn't adore her all the more for it. This wasn't simple. This was drowning in complicated. The fact that she understood and wasn't pushing meant the world to him. Because he wanted to throw caution to the wind, and to be honest, his ability to do the right thing was wearing thin.

"Tell you something? What do you want to know?"

"How about you match mine with your answers?"

He considered this as he set their plates at the table and brought around silverware, while Lila brought their drinks.

"All right, let's see. I'm a dog person, too. Obviously." Henry groaned as though he knew they were talking about him and rolled over, then immediately fell back asleep. "I'll eat any fish or seafood, but count me out for sushi or raw oysters."

"So you've had them or you just don't like them?" Lila asked, taking a bite of her fajita, but then her eyes widened and she made a moaning sound as she enjoyed the bite, then swallowed. "Oh my God. These are the best fajitas I've ever had."

"I know." Suddenly Charlie couldn't pull his gaze from her mouth.

She laughed. "Cocky, huh?"

"No, it's just I met a guy when I lived in the Keys that gave me the recipe. I can't really take credit for it."

She took another bite and closed her eyes. "Wow. So good. That's two meals you've spoiled me with. Next time I have to cook for you."

"Do you cook?"

"No, not at all. What I meant by cooking was having Annie cook something for me and then I'd present it as though I cooked it myself. I'm very honest like that."

Charlie burst into laughter, but stopped when he realized she was watching him. "Now who's staring?"

"I can't help it. You're really hot. It's hard for a woman to look away."

Charlie flashed a crooked grin, curious where this honesty was coming from, and that was when he noticed she'd drained her wine glass.

He pointed at the glass. "How many of those have you had?"

"Just two. No, three." Her eyes searched around as though the number could be conjured from the air, and he chuckled again. "Didn't realize you were such a cheap drunk."

"Hey! I'm not. Okay, maybe a little. And you didn't finish the list."

Taking another pull of his beer, he set it down and thought through what Lila had said before. "Well, I already told you the Lucas thing. I couldn't be prouder of him. He's a hero. A real, living, breathing hero. But, yeah, I miss him. I'm glad I moved back, though. Lets me see him more often." He downed his beer, pausing to think through what he would say for his final revelation. Anything he said about his current thoughts and feelings would only elevate things, and he didn't want to offer any more to her if he couldn't deliver. She deserved more.

So instead, he leaned back in his chair and peered over at her, the story coming to him like it had happened yesterday. "You remember the Halloween at the farm? When we were in high school?"

Immediately, her body tensed and she reached for her wine glass again, but Charlie pushed it back. She was cute when she was buzzed, but he didn't want her to feel sick tomorrow.

"I remember it," she said finally, but she wasn't looking at him now.

For a moment, he wondered if he'd chosen the right story. Would she hear him out? "And do you remember when we were over at your house earlier that day?"

"In the hammock," she said, tracing her wine glass with her fingertip.

Charlie pressed on. Now or never. "I wanted to kiss you that day. I wanted it so badly it took every ounce of strength in me to pull away. And I did, but I couldn't shake that moment from my head. I'd known you most of my life, and somewhere along the way, I stopped thinking of you as Lucas's sister and started thinking of you as . . . more. So much more."

Her eyes met his then, a smile hidden within them, and now this was the hard part. How would she react? Would she push him away, get angry, understand?

"That day I left you and went to talk to Lucas. I mentioned you, a bit of what was in my head, and he flipped." Charlie reached for his beer, took another pull, but the damn thing was empty. He set it back down, considered getting another, but then—

"Charlie?"

"*Hmm*?"

"Finish the story."

He sighed as he caught the hurt on her face. "He told me I wasn't to touch you, that you deserved more and he was right. I knew he was right. And I also knew you had to have felt what I felt in that hammock. It was. . . ."

"Overwhelming."

He locked on her. "Life changing. I didn't know how to make you stay away from me, to realize that Lucas was right, you deserved more. Better. Then Audrey came up to me and told me your plans to tell me how you felt. I knew if you said it first, I'd never be able to turn you away, so I . . ."

"So you faked a hookup."

Guilt punched him in the gut, and he wished he'd chosen a different story. Something that didn't end with Lila in tears. "Yes, but I—"

"Shut up." She pushed out of her chair, and Charlie was almost desperate now. He stood, ready to say he was sorry, he'd been a stupid teen. Hell, he was stupid now. Whatever to make her sit back down, to not disappear on him again.

"You don't understand, I—"

"Stop talking."

Shit, what the hell had he done? He opened his mouth to try again, when she stopped before him, and he thought this was it, she was going to slap him and leave, all the hope he had for something more gone because of a stupid story.

Then instead she said, "You liked me, too?"

Charlie shook his head in confusion. "Like you? You don't get it, do you? I have never seen anyone the way I see you."

And then she went to him, her lips on his, and he lost all control. That brief moment of fear that she'd leave, and of the subsequent emptiness, was enough for him. He was already gone, sailed away, his heart turned over to this woman. But really, she'd had his heart since she was a girl, and he'd never gotten it back. There were a thousand reasons they shouldn't be together, but maybe that didn't matter. Maybe all they needed was one reason that they should.

He lifted her up, her legs wrapping around his waist, and all thoughts, all hope for him doing the right thing flew out the window. If she wanted him, he wouldn't push her away.

Chapter Eighteen

A shudder worked through Lila's body as Charlie gently laid her back against his bed. He took a step back and stared down at her, like he couldn't believe this was his reality, and that look in his eyes, so full of want and care for her, made her eager to show him how deeply he'd seeped into her heart, burrowing in her soul.

She lifted up and reached for his belt buckle, slowly unbuckling it, then unbuttoning his jeans.

"Lila . . ."

She pressed a finger to her lips. "*Shhh.*" And then she pushed his jeans and boxers to the ground, and his length, long and hard and eager, stood out before her. She gripped his thick shaft and slowly stroked, her eyes on his, before she licked her lips and then wrapped her mouth around him. A hiss rushed out of his mouth and reflexively he pumped his hips once, needing to be deeper, and she was happy to oblige. Gripping him harder, she licked down the length of him, tasting his saltiness, and then sucking the end, before doing it again, toying with him.

"Jesus Christ," he said, and she peeked up at him to find his face twisted in pleasure, the look so unbelievably hot that it gave Lila the courage to play. Reaching down she stroked his balls, and then sucked him in deeper, tasting every inch of him, and loving every second of it. She was pleasuring him, and yet she herself was wet, so close to coming that she could barely contain herself.

Charlie's hand threaded into her hair and he gripped her head, guiding her as she took him in again and again, She moaned around him, so absorbed in it that she thought she might lose herself right then, when he pulled out and lifted her shirt over her head, dropping it to the floor.

"Not yet." He helped her stand, pushed her shorts down, and slowly stroked her, before sliding a finger inside her. "God, you're so wet. Perfect." He gently laid her back against his bed and started for her. "I want you so badly it's killing me right now, but if this is too much, too fast . . . If you want me to stop—"

"If you stop now, I'll never speak to you again."

A chuckle broke from his lips, and she reached out to him, her hand on his cheek, and though she was so turned on, so ready, she couldn't stop the surge of emotions spiraling through her. Because this wasn't just attraction and lust. This was Charlie and he was everything to her, and finally, after all this time, he was hers. The realization was too much.

"I need you to touch me," she said, the words barely above a moan.

"Like this?" He pressed a kiss to her ankle, then slowly trailed his tongue up her calf. "Or this." Another kiss, this one inside her thigh, and Lila's eyes closed as she writhed under his touch. "Or this."

Hot breath danced across her hip, then his mouth covered her mound, and a moan slipped from her lips, so eager she was close to begging. His tongue went to work, licking and stroking, and she gripped his shoulders, desperate now. "Please . . ."

Charlie licked his lips as he pulled back, his eyes full of wickedness and want, and then he pulled open the nightstand drawer and took out a condom. "Let's see if Double Ecstasy does what it claims."

Lila scanned the condom wrapper and laughed. "You didn't."

"Hell yeah, I did."

He rolled it on, and all humor fell from Lila's face as she drank him in. Each taut muscle. The small line of light hair that trailed from his belly button. The sharp *V* of his pelvic muscle. God, he was unbelievably sexy.

Climbing over her now, he lowered himself until his body pressed against hers, and then that delicious mouth of his went to her neck, her collarbone, her breasts. He sucked on one of her nipples, then bit down lightly, and that was enough.

"Charlie . . . God . . . please."

Without another word, he drove inside her hard, nothing gentle about it, and she held onto him as he watched her. Then, when he knew he'd found her sweet spot, he sped up, faster, harder, so damn deep, and then she burst all around him, vibrating in spasms. And then he covered her mouth with his, her taste still on his lips as he groaned, and released inside her. His breathing was heavy as he laid down beside her, their bodies intertwined.

"That was . . ." He released another breath, and Lila could feel his heart pounding against his chest.

"Amazing."

He kissed her again. "I'm done, you know that, right? It's only you for me."

Lila nuzzled against him. "Promise?"

"If you'll let me, I'll give you the world. Everything I have and everything I am. It's yours."

Lila's heart became light, the words right there, three words to convey what he meant to her, but then she heard his breathing slow, his body relaxing, and she peered up to find his eyes closed.

"I love you," she whispered. And though she knew he didn't hear her, she fell asleep with a smile on her face.

Chapter Nineteen

Charlie woke to the smell of freshly laundered clothes and sunshine, warmth pressed against his chest, and a sense of contentment and purpose he hadn't felt in a long time. Maybe not ever.

He thought of that day in the hammock, his chest so full he thought it would explode, the desire to kiss her so strong he'd nearly lost it and thrown caution to the wind and leaned in. But he hadn't. And now, more than a decade later, here she was, in his arms.

They'd spent most of the night exploring one another. The first time was fast, a rush of hormones and emotions. But then he woke an hour later and traced lazy circles on her stomach, then her legs, and suddenly she was awake, too. She climbed on top of him, but this time it was slower, their bodies coming together, a new understanding forming between them. And so the night went on like that, reaching for each other, sleeping a little, then starting it all over again, like a fantasy come true.

Not wanting to open his eyes, he pulled her closer, tucking her against him, her slow, sleepy breaths warming him all over again. This was the real thing, right here, and unless God made him, he would never let her go. He kissed her cheek, prepared to try to fall back asleep, when a knock at his door, followed by another, had him groaning.

"Go away," he called, then he realized the person could be the cops here to update them on the attacker. Slipping his arm out from under Lila, he climbed out of bed and pulled on a pair of gym shorts, then turned to look at her. Her dark hair spread across his white pillow, his sheet tangled around her legs and covered her bare breasts. God, she was beautiful. Smart and kind and funny—perfect. And she was his. The thought made him happier than he deserved to be, and he could stay there, watching her sleep all day. But then the knocking started up again, and he drew a breath for patience. This better be important.

Reaching the door, Charlie unlocked the deadbolt and opened it up, prepared to either tell one of his brothers to come later or to ask the officer to step outside so they could talk. But it wasn't Zac or Brady or an officer.

It was Lucas.

"Uh, hey!" Charlie said, his voice too high, his brain still foggy from his and Lila's night of exploration. He closed the door and stepped outside, unsure what else to do, but he needed Lucas far, far away from here. At least until Lila left or at the very least put clothes on. Then they could explain this to him together. That this wasn't a fling; it was more. It was everything. She was everything.

"What are you doing?" Lucas asked. "I went to see Lila at Annie's and she explained to me what was going on. Said Lila was staying here until they caught the bastard."

Shit. Of course he would go see Lila first and hear where she was, and then there was the Honda Pilot in his driveway, obvious to anyone with half-decent sight.

"Right, yeah. She's here, but she's asleep, so I didn't want to wake her." All the truth, but Lucas stared at him like he could decode the deeper meaning in his words. Charlie drew a long breath, then two. Twenty-plus years of friendship meant they could read each other better than anyone, and if it was anything else, Charlie would have already unloaded the full story. The full, true story. But this wasn't something else. It was Lila. And he was tired of trying to do the right thing by Lucas while destroying Lila in the process. He wouldn't do that, not again.

So with that in mind, he sighed heavily, and forced himself to look his best friend in the eye. "Look, man, we need to talk. I—"

But before he could continue, his door opened and Lila stood there, wearing one of Charlie's shirts and nothing else. "Hey, I didn't know where you—" She stopped as her eyes found Lucas, but he wasn't looking at her anymore. He was looking at Charlie.

"You didn't."

"Let me explain."

"Let you freaking explain? I ask you to protect my sister, and you take that as an invitation to take advantage of her?" He started for

Charlie, but Lila stepped between them first, her hands braced on her brother's chest as she lightly pushed him back.

"Stop."

Lucas's face turned red with anger, but he took a step back. "This is between Charlie and me."

"No, actually, it isn't. It's between *me* and Charlie. Not you."

He shook his head, so angry now that Charlie knew if Lila wasn't standing between them, fists would be thrown.

"Look, we wanted to talk to you about this," Charlie said. "Once you were back here and safe. This isn't some casual hookup."

A sarcastic laugh broke from his lips as he scowled at Charlie. "Right. Because you know so much about serious relationships. About commitment. How many have you had over the years? Oh that's right. None. What evidence is there that you would take this seriously, that you would treat her the way she deserves to be treated? There is none!"

"I get that you're angry, but if you could let me explain I—"

"Explain?" Lucas tossed his hands in the air. "There is no explanation. I trusted you! And you what, lead my baby sister into your bed?"

Lila's hands clenched into fists as she lifted her head to face off with her brother. "I'm not a baby. I haven't been a baby in a long, long time, and it's time you stop treating me like I am one. I get that you love our family, that you feel it's your job to look after all of us. I get that and I respect it. But I am an adult, and I make my own choices. And I choose Charlie."

"You're vulnerable right now. You don't know what you want."

"Lucas, look at me," Lila said, and he placed his hands on his hips before forcing himself to look at her. "Now listen to me when I tell you this. Actually listen. I love him," she said. "I have loved him since I was old enough to even know the meaning of the word, and now I've gotten to know the man he is, and I love him even more." She turned to Charlie then. "I love you, and I know we're not ready for those words, but I feel it and I can't help it. I do."

Charlie took her hand and pressed it to his lips, his mouth open to say it back, to tell her that she rebuilt his heart. That he never thought he'd care about anything again, not in any real, concrete way. But he cared about her, and now, more than anything, he wanted to give her the life she deserved.

But Lucas spoke up before he could say any of those things.

"This isn't happening. She's a doctor! She should marry another doctor or a lawyer or someone who is on her level."

Ah, and now it was all becoming clear. "On her level? Right, so what you're saying is someone who is good enough for her, because obviously I'm not."

Lucas's jaw ground together as he stared at Charlie. "No, you're not. You're a man who promised to protect her while I was gone, and I come back to find out you let that piece of shit get to her, get into her apartment. You decided it was more important to get her into your bed than to protect her."

And Charlie didn't know why, but those words from his best friend, from a man he had always considered a brother, tore through him. Of course she could do better. Of course. But he'd be damned if he would allow Lucas to claim that Charlie had been reckless with her safety.

"I guess that's it, then," Charlie said.

"Yeah, it is. Sorry, but you aren't dating my sister."

Now Charlie's own anger rose up inside him. He reached out to take Lila's hand. "Actually, I meant that you've said your piece. I hoped you'd support this, that maybe you'd be happy for us. Your best friend with your sister. Why wouldn't you be okay with it? I own a successful business. I am financially stable, debt free, I always have been. You know this about me. What exactly about me isn't good enough? But then I guess that's the real problem: In your eyes, I've never been on your level either, have I?"

Lucas looked away, and Charlie had his answer.

"Enough," Lila said. "You're both just angry. You can't end your friendship over this. I won't let you. Lucas, I love you. I will always respect you and your opinion, but I can care for whomever I like. You have no jurisdiction over my love life. This is my decision, and I pick him."

Charlie kissed Lila, and Lucas stormed off. Twenty-plus years of friendship . . . over.

Chapter Twenty

Charlie and Lila both fell into silence as they got ready for the day, until Lila went to meet Lucas for lunch and then it was Charlie, alone in an empty house. He wanted to drive her into town, but showing up together would only make things worse. But how much worse could it be?

He would head into Southern Dive to open the shop, so he showered, then put on his clothes, made coffee, all of the tasks mindlessly done because his thoughts were all on what Lucas had said . . . and how right he had been. His thoughts drifted back to their upbringings and how different they had been. Charlie's family wasn't poor by any stretch of the imagination, but they weren't wealthy either. They weren't educated. Everyone in Lucas and Lila's family graduated from college, Lucas while serving. And Lila was a doctor. Charlie might run a successful business now, and certainly the farm was doing well, but he was as blue collar as a Southern man could be. Lila was anything but blue collar.

And then there was the issue of the attacker getting into Lila's apartment, and while Charlie felt he'd watched out for Lila maybe he was wrong. Maybe he should have done more. What if Lila had been there when the attacker was there? Anything could have happened and then—

No, he wouldn't let himself go down that road. She was safe. But Charlie had allowed his feelings for her to overcome his logic, and maybe that slip was why he missed the attacker coming to Crestler's Key, photographing them together, and then getting into her apartment.

Arriving at Southern Dive, he unlocked the door, turned off the alarm, and turned on the lights, each step dragging him deeper into the black hole that was taking over his head and heart. He woke his laptop and went to work checking online orders. The numbers of questions about T-shirt designs and custom requests were increasing to the point now that Charlie had an autoreply setup that announced the T-shirt line was in development, to stay tuned for news. But that reply had been in place for three months now, and he was no closer to starting the T-shirt line. The process, which he'd discussed briefly with his lawyer, involved patents, which took time to approve, then finding a good screen printer to produce the shirts, then packaging and pricing, and the list went on forever.

Still, as he stared at the ten orders, all of them inquiring about the shirts, all since yesterday, he wondered if maybe... But then he thought of who he was, his experience. What business did he have trying to create a business from the ground up all on his own? Southern Dive had been different. He had his brothers there to help.

Frustrated, he closed the laptop and was preparing to go through the shop when a soft knock at the main door pulled his attention away. Immediately, his eyes locked on Lila's through the glass, and he started over, every step like his shoes were filled with lead. Because he knew where this was going, what he had to do.

"Hey," she said, as he unlocked the door, and then she wrapped her arms around his neck, but he couldn't bring himself to hug her back. That would only make this harder. She pulled away, her face pinched in concern. "Are you okay?"

"Any news on the attacker?" he asked, hoping to change the subject.

"No, nothing new. They want me to be watched, but Lucas said he would handle it. You know how he is."

Overprotective, Charlie wanted to say, but then wasn't he overprotective, too? Weren't we all when it came to the ones we loved?

"Yeah, I do. How did lunch go?"

She sighed heavily. "As good as expected. He doesn't understand."

"Right." Charlie turned away and went back to the T-shirt wall, where he'd decided to pull every stack off and reorganize them. Because apparently he wanted to torture himself.

"What are you doing?" Lila asked.

"Organizing the shelf."

"No. What are you doing?"

Unable to avoid it any longer he spun to face her, his frustration taking over logical thought. "I don't know what the hell I'm doing! I want to be with you. I've wanted it for as long as I can remember. But every single thing Lucas said was right. I'm not . . . you're . . . I just don't know how this can work. And now I've ruined the only real friendship I have."

Lila nodded slowly, her face etched in anger, and Charlie wanted to go to her, to apologize, take it all back. But he couldn't, because deep down he knew this was the right thing.

"You know, when you stood up to him at your house, I thought 'Finally! Finally, Charlie is done being in Lucas's shadow and will put my arrogant, thinks-he-can-do-no-wrong brother in his place.' But clearly not. Didn't it ever occur to you that you are everything I ever wanted, too? That I'm proud of you? That everything you touch takes off and flies? You don't need a degree to be intelligent and driven. Those things are already inside of you, and that's why if you decide to create your T-shirt line, I know it's going to blow up, too. And not because Zac helps you or Brady pushes it or all those followers you have on social media tell everyone they know. It's because of you. Because you are amazing." Her lip trembled and she dropped her gaze to the hardwood floors, and Charlie took a step toward her. "But I can't make you want to fight for me. I can't make you put me first. I can't . . ." Her voice shook.

Charlie wished she would deck him right now, because he deserved it. Everything she was saying was right, but he couldn't make sense of this in his head. Losing someone you care about to gain someone else. Nothing about this was right.

Finally, she focused on him again, her eyes red, but she was holding back her tears. "I'm not a girl anymore. I'm a woman, and love is only a small part of a relationship. You need to trust each other and know the other person isn't going to back out on you when things get tough. And I just don't . . . I'm not sure I can say that about you. So, I'll make this easy for you. Good-bye, Charlie."

She turned around and walked out the door, her head down as she started down the sidewalk, and every fiber in Charlie's body ached to go after her. To beg and plead and say she was right, he was an idiot. But he couldn't. So instead, he turned back to his shelf, the pile of shirts there, and grabbed the lot of them and threw them back onto the shelf. Then he grabbed his keys, shut out the lights, and walked out—alone.

The tears refused to stop, despite all Lila's efforts to tell them to stop. It was like she'd been promised the future she wanted, got a small peek into what it would look like, and then she woke from the dream only to realize it had never been a possibility in the first place. Her heart hurt, and all she wanted to do was go back to Southern Dive and ask him to try, to talk to Lucas with her. And then talk to Lucas again, and again, until he—

Oh my God. What was she thinking? Lucas was her brother, not her father, and even then, she was a twenty-eight-year-old woman. What right did anyone have to involve themselves in her love life? They didn't! *He* didn't!

So with renewed anger, Lila turned her car around and sped toward her brother's house, each second making her madder and madder until she feared her brother might not survive this visit. She slammed her Pilot into park in his driveway. Immediately, he opened his screen door, was already through it, asking what was wrong, when she flew out of her car, stomping and ready to push him to the ground, like when they were kids and he'd rip the head off one of her Barbie dolls.

"I am not a little girl anymore."

His face switched from worry to confusion. "I know that."

"Do you? Because this is all your fault. You treat me like a freaking porcelain doll, always have, and then the attack happened, and it's a thousand times worse. Charlie is your best friend. The best man you know, and you treated him like he was nothing. All for what? Because I fell for him? News flash, I fell for him a long time ago, and you had no right getting involved. It's my life, mine. My decision."

Lucas took a step back. "I just want what's best for you."

"What's best for me is Charlie."

He stared at her. "I know him, know the way he thinks. You should hear the way he talks about women."

Lila crossed her arms and glared at her brother. "Really, when? As an adult?"

"Well . . ."

"Because it sounds like you're talking about a sixteen-year-old boy, with more hormones than brains. But that isn't Charlie, and you know it. He's not a boy now. He's a man. A good man. A great man, in fact, and I don't think he would say anything bad about anybody. That's not who he is. And he's smart, ridiculously smart. He's built multiple businesses now, all on his own, and he's about to launch a third that's probably going to make him wealthier than either of us have a chance of being. And you know what? He won't even care. It won't change him, because he's that good of a person. You've called him your best friend for all these years, but you're not a friend. A real friend doesn't treat someone this way." She started for her car, then paused and turned back. "You should be ashamed of yourself. I am."

And then she got back into her car, shut the door, and put the car in reverse. It took all of two seconds for her phone to ring, and for her to peer down and see Lucas's name. Her gaze lifted to find him still standing in the driveway, his hands lifted in surrender.

She put the car in park again and got out. "What now?"

"You're right," he said, shaking his head. "The things I see, the things I do . . . I just, it has changed me. Continues to change me. I worry about you. You're my little sister. But you're right. I'm not being fair, and Charlie . . ." He trailed off, and Lila took a step toward him, her arms crossed. But they were family. You didn't turn your back on family. You didn't run. You yelled and screamed, threw things if you must, but then you forgave each other.

"Don't tell me. Tell him. Because he'll never admit it, but he's hurting right now, and it's your fault."

Lucas looked uncomfortable, and Lila almost laughed. "I'm not asking you guys to go cry it out. Just call him or go see him. Say you're sorry."

"And what will you do? Wyatt is out there somewhere. You can't go back to your apartment. Can you just stay here? Please. I'll go see Charlie, bring him back with me."

Lila's eyes found the grass. "Actually, I think that's over now."

"Over what I said? Hell no. I'm going to talk to him."

"I don't think it'll matter. Honestly, I respect that he wants to do the right thing by you, but I want a man who would never push me away, no matter what. No matter who was between us."

Lucas put an arm around her and pulled her close. "Go on in, make yourself at home, and I'll be back in an hour. With Charlie."

She opened her mouth to argue, when Lucas said, "Trust me."

Chapter Twenty-one

Charlie grabbed a beer from his fridge and kicked back on his couch, his thoughts on Lila and what he was doing. He pictured her face again, the hurt there, and he wanted to chuck the beer across the room. Was he really so scared of giving himself over to someone that he wasn't willing to take a risk? Because deep down, he knew this wasn't just about Lucas.

Everything that happened with Jade had messed up his thinking about relationships and women in general. It was hard to trust someone, and add to that the issues surrounding Lila and the strain on his friendship with Lucas, and the whole thing reeked of failure and pain. Plus, if he started things with Lila and they ended, he would lose both of them for good. That much was certain. Though maybe he already had.

Closing his eyes, he tried to order his brain to think through a solution, and when that didn't work he prayed for one, hoping the Great Man could give him the answer he needed. But when he opened his eyes, it was still just him in his house, no epic revelation or answer. He had to figure this out on his own.

Needing something to do, he stood up, unsure what he was doing, and his gaze caught on the shelf beside his TV, where one of his yearbooks was set out. He walked over and checked the year. It was his senior year, Lila's sophomore. And the start of guys noticing her the way he'd been noticing her for years. She must have taken it out when she was there earlier. He flipped it open to her year, and then to the *J*s, and there she was staring back at him, younger, for sure, and yet she looked exactly the same. Dark hair, beautiful blue eyes, a hint of a tan, huge smile. And then he noticed the note written in the margin in black sharpie. A note that hadn't been there before.

I loved you then, and I love you now.
Thanks for being you.
— L

God, he was a moron. A giant, stupid, freaking moron. But he knew what he needed to do now, and he wasn't about to let Lucas or even his own doubts get in the way. Because he didn't just care for Lila, he loved her. Deep down in his bones, so much it hurt to even consider going on without her. That kind of love needed to be nurtured and allowed to thrive and grow. They might not make it—hell no one knew the future—but he had to try. He would regret it for the rest of his life if he didn't.

Grabbing his keys, he threw open his door only to slam into Lucas.

"What the hell?" Charlie said, startling back. "What are you doing here?"

Lucas eyed his keys, then him. "Where were you going?"

Charlie glared at his best friend. "To get your sister, whether you like it or not. I love her. This isn't a game for me. It's my life, and I want her in it, and if she'll give me a second chance, then I'll be damned if you're going to stand in the way."

A slow smile crept across Lucas's face. "Finally."

"What?" Charlie spit out, growing more frustrated by the second.

Lucas motioned inside the house. "Can I come in for a second?"

"You're not going to talk me out of this." Charlie knew what he wanted now, and every second they stood here talking about it meant one more second away from Lila and his future.

"Look, I'm sorry I was an ass before. Seriously. I was out of line. I think I wanted you to want it enough to fight for her. Then I'd know it was real for you. Sure, I was worried. Sure, I was being a dick. But inside, I just wanted to know you cared enough to not hurt her. I can see that you do now, and she loves you. I'm happy for you, man. Both of you."

"Yeah, you've got a jacked up way of showing it."

"Well, I'm done with that. And I shouldn't have said that you're not good enough. You're my best friend, always have been, always will be. But right now, Lila is hurting and it's both of our faults, not just mine. So I was hoping I could convince you to go with me to talk to her."

"Where is she?"

"My house."

Charlie shot his friend a look. "And we're good? Because I'm not trying to get in the car with you just so you can axe me and dump my body in Lake Cherokee or something."

Lucas released a booming laugh. "Tempting, but nah, we're good. I'll still kick your ass if you hurt her."

"I'll kick my own ass if I hurt her."

Lucas's brow furrowed. "We seriously need to work on your comebacks."

Charlie laughed, his chest lighter now. One down, one to go. "Duly noted, thanks." Then he pushed past his friend.

"Where are you going?"

"To get my girl."

A grin flashed on Lucas's face. "Jeep's still running. Hop in."

Lila peeked out the foyer window, then walked around to the kitchen, then came back to the window. Still nothing. Nearly an hour had passed, and Lucas still wasn't back with Charlie, which could only mean that Charlie didn't want to come for her, right? What other explanation could there be?

An accident?

A long conversation between the two where they made up and caught up on old times? Maybe.

But deep down, Lila knew Charlie's insecurities about them were too great for him to take a chance, and if he didn't want to take a chance, if he didn't want to try, then . . .

She grabbed a blanket from the back of Lucas's couch, wrapped it around her shoulders, and stepped outside onto the porch, needing some fresh air. And needing to do something to occupy her mind. Because right then, she felt . . . hopeless. How could one day change so much between them?

Last night had been amazing, out of this world, beyond her wildest dreams amazing. And now all she could think about was what she could have done differently, what she could have said to convince

Charlie that they were worth a little bump in the road with Lucas. That she wasn't Jade, wouldn't steal his things and his dog. But then those thoughts made her sad, too, because if he were the right man, her soul mate, then she wouldn't have to convince him to want her.

Even though it wasn't night yet, the moon shined down from above, the sun dropping away, and soon darkness would be there, and with it would come all those feelings of hurt she'd been avoiding. Because for as long as she could remember, she had wanted Charlie Littleton, and though she'd suffered pain at his hand before, this was different. This wasn't childhood crushes and misunderstandings. This was real adult stuff, and frankly, Lila didn't want any part of it. Times like these, she wished life was like a book, where you could skim over the bad parts and reread the good parts over and over, experiencing them all over again. But life wasn't a book or movie. It was hard, with real challenges and real pain. Something Lila kept learning the hard way.

A shiver worked down her spine as the wind picked up. The weather had called for a cold front that would bring daytime temperatures down to the mid-fifties and night temps into the forties. Apparently the front was here, which meant it was time for her cold-natured self to go back into the house.

She had just turned around to go inside when a sharp sound from her left pulled her attention away from the door. One step in the direction of the sound, then two, and then a loud bang, followed by sharp pain from the back of her head, and then the world around her became blurry.

All at once, her instincts kicked in and she whipped around, her fists poised to protect her, but she couldn't focus past the throbbing in her head. Warm liquid trailed down her neck, cueing her into two hard truths—she was bleeding and someone had hit her from behind.

And that was when she saw the dark figure walk around from the left side of the wrap-around back deck, and every fiber in Lila's body screamed for her to run.

Flashes hit in her mind. A nice, kind smile. A trusting voice. Easy conversation. Warm hand on her back as they walked into the restaurant for their first date. Nothing about their encounters had hinted at danger. But then the third date she went to the bathroom, came back, and suddenly her vision was blurry, her thoughts clouded.

"Ready to go?" he'd asked, saying he had an early meeting the next day. They walked back to his car and then . . .

"Hello, Lila," Wyatt said, each word drawn out, his tone as soft as ever. Like they were old friends being reunited, instead of what they were—attacker and victim.

Lila took a step back, her hand tightening around her cell phone, but she couldn't make a call without looking at her phone, and she refused to lose focus on the danger before her. One wrong move, and he could have her again, and then, then . . .

Her breathing escalated as terror ripped through her. *Come on, Lucas, come home. Help me,* she thought, and then she remembered something Charlie had said to her when they were camping—she wasn't a victim. She wasn't helpless. He had failed.

He had failed.

And though she didn't consider herself weak when the first attack occurred, she did consider herself naïve. Well, not anymore. Her defenses were up, her body toned and ready to fight. And this time, she knew who the monster was, and he was staring her straight in the face.

Wyatt took a tentative step toward her. "This doesn't have to be hard."

"Is that what you said to the other girls?" Lila asked, allowing her anger to overcome her fear. She took another step back. But she knew this house well, had visited numerous times when Lucas had it built, and she was near the end of the back deck, which meant she had two options—fight or run.

He stopped mid-step and cocked his head. "How do you know about them? Were you checking up on me? Seeing what has my interest. That sounds an awful lot like affection."

"Affection?" Lila spit out. "You took those girls. Where are they?"

A smile curled his lips. "Elsewhere."

"But they're alive?" Lila's heartbeat sped up, a plan forming. If she could keep him talking, get him to admit where he'd taken the girls, then maybe she could help ensure their rescue.

"Now, now, why would I kill them until I find the perfect replacement?"

Her eyebrows pulled together, and she realized that all three of them—she and the two women he'd taken—all had similar features. Dark hair, blue eyes, light skin. This new piece of information mixed with something else he had told her when they first started emailing. He was a widower; his wife had died in a car crash two years before he and Lila met. *The perfect replacement . . .*

"Your wife, what did she look like?"

He paused again. "My wife? How did you—Oh . . ." Realization crossed his face, and she knew he was remembering what he'd told her. But instead of the mention of his wife throwing him off, his face twisted, the smile deepening, his eyes slanting up, making him appear all the more evil. He took a step now. "Dark brown hair." Another step. "Blue eyes." Closer. "Fair skin." Lila's chest tightened, fear taking over. "Just. Like. You."

And then he lunged for her, just as she scrambled back, falling over the back railing of the deck and landing hard in the mulch below. Wood chips cut into her hands, but she pushed aside the pain and scrambled to her feet.

Then he grabbed her from behind. "Nah ah, beautiful lady. I have you just where I want you now."

But he didn't know what Lila knew. That she had suffered through countless lessons with her brother when he visited her, then a private instructor in Charlotte, all to teach her exactly what to do when someone larger than her had her in his control. She bent down and threw her head back as hard as she could, knocking him in the face, then spun out of his hold, right as car lights shined out from the driveway to the woods behind them. She started to run just as Wyatt grabbed her, pulled out a gun, and pressed the barrel to her temple. "Don't move. Or I will kill you. Do you understand?"

Lila nodded slowly, her salvation so close and yet so far out of reach.

"Good girl."

The sounds of car doors opening pierced the silence, followed by footsteps. Lila said a prayer that they would come this way, but then she heard the front door open, the screen door slap shut, and then voices.

"Tiny, where are you?" Lucas called.

"Was she here when you left?" Lila's eyes closed at the sound of

Charlie's voice, her heart warming with the smallest bit of relief. *Please, I'm here. Out here.* "Did you make sure she was okay?"

"Calm down. She's here somewhere. Her car's out front."

A slow breath worked through Lila's lungs. Her car! They knew she was here.

"Then where could she—"

There was silence from inside the house, and Lila wondered what was happening when Lucas spoke up again. "I bet she called Audrey to come get her, girl time or something. I'll call Audrey and check." Silence again, followed by, "Audrey, hey, it's Lucas . . ." The words became muffled, and Wyatt tightened his grip around her and started dragging her back, but all she could think was *No, not again.*

Without thinking, she stomped hard on his foot and spun out of his hold, just as he raised his gun, and Lila's heart stopped, time standing still, her life flashing before her eyes, but instead of a gunshot ringing out, another voice, a voice she'd recognize anywhere said, "Drop it, now."

Wyatt's mouth curved up into a sick grin. "Hello, Charlie. I wondered if I would meet you."

Charlie cocked his head. "Yeah, I wondered if I'd meet you, too. You know, you behind bars, me on the other side while you're introduced to Big Al. I'm sure you can imagine what Big Al's greatest talents are." In the time Charlie had told his small story, distracting Wyatt, Lila had taken a step toward him, closer to safety. "And you're going to rot there like the scum you are," Charlie continued. "I'll make sure of it."

"Yeah, you and what army?" Wyatt asked.

"Me." And then before any of them could react, Lucas leaped over the back deck, landed, and then immediately crushed his foot into Wyatt's chest, throwing him backward, the gun flying out of his hand. And then Charlie was over Wyatt, gun poised, when Lila rushed to them.

"Don't shoot him!"

The man she loved turned to look at her. "Why the hell not?"

Wyatt shook on the ground, his hands out. "I'll—"

"Shut it," Charlie and Lucas said at the same time. Lucas was beside Charlie now, both men towering over Wyatt, ready to end this if he made a wrong move.

"If you kill him, they will never find those two women. Please."

Just then sirens sounded in the distance, drawing near, until two police cars were in the driveway and then four cops were out, guns raised. One yelled, "Drop the weapon!"

Charlie dropped his gun and turned, hands up; Lucas did the same. The officers approached and handcuffed Wyatt, while Lucas explained what had happened. And as though everything, the rush of it, the fear hit her at once, Lila faced Charlie, tears in her eyes and he started for her.

"Don't cry, Tiny girl. I'm here." He pulled her to him and wrapped his arms around her. "And I'm never letting you go again."

Chapter Twenty-two

Charlie gripped Lila's hand as they walked out along the river bank, fishing poles in her other hand, tackle box and cooler in his. Two days had passed since the attack at Lucas's, and Charlie had asked Lila what he could do to take her mind off things, and she had said, "Take me camping. I want to out-fish you." So with a grin, he closed down Southern Dive, packed up his camping gear, and here they were.

The stream ran alongside them, bubbling and rushing over rocks, while birds called out a melody from somewhere in the trees. It was peaceful, perfect. Just like their first time, and hopefully this would be one of many more to come.

"And they found the women?" he asked as he set down the tackle box and small cooler.

She nodded. "He had them in his basement. Had a hidden room down there. I guess that was where he had me, too. I gave another statement, and investigators feel they have enough to put him away for good this time."

Her eyes diverted, and Charlie tilted her chin up so she would look at him again. "I can't imagine how hard this is, but I'll be there for you every step of the way. You have no idea how brave you've been. You helped find these women, helped save them. Because of you, they get to have full lives. Don't you see that?"

"I just . . . I want them to be safe. I want Wyatt behind bars. I don't want him to use his money to escape."

"That won't happen. There's too much evidence this time."

She released a long breath. "I hope you're right."

"Listen, this is over now. He failed because of you. He failed with all three of you, because of you. He's going to jail, where he'll never be able to hurt you again. But if by some miracle he gets out and tries to come for you, then he has to go through me. I'll take out the bastard myself. Because I will be damned if he touches someone I love again. I will—"

Lila's hand went to his arm, stopping him mid-rant. "Wait, what did you say?"

Charlie's eyes fell on her, a slow smile spreading on his face. "I said I love you. I should have told you before, I should have shouted it to anyone who would listen, but then the attack happened, and I didn't know if you were ready to hear it. I wanted to give you time, but God . . ." He ran a hand over her face and cupped her cheek. "Every time I look at you, I feel like my heart is going to burst and my thoughts get jumbled, and . . ." He stopped. "Say something."

Her face lit. "You love me?"

"Are you crazy? I love you so much it's killing me."

Then she launched herself into his arms, her lips on his. "I love you, too. So, so much." Then her smile turned sly. "And just remember that when I out-fish you today."

They broke into laughter and spent the next two hours fishing, lost in the beauty around them, no worries but this moment and how they'd finally found their happily ever after, together.

Always.

Epilogue

One year later

"Darlin', what are you doing in there? We've got movers arriving in . . . crap, they're here now."

Lila stared at the bathroom door to her and Charlie's new house, white with country-style detailing. They'd built the house from the ground up, picked out every detail, including the custom-made door she was presently standing behind.

They'd snuck off to get married three months prior, a private ceremony with only immediate family, up in the mountains, by the river that had cemented their relationship from the start. And Lila loved Charlie. She loved him so fully that she knew for the rest of her life she would be happy, safe, and loved.

But as her gaze returned to the small white stick in her hand, two definite pink lines clear in the view window, she wondered what would happen now.

She had just taken over the animal hospital, Baxter finally retiring so he could focus on his golf game. Charlie had just launched his T-shirt business, with orders coming in so fast they could hardly keep up. Everything was great, wonderful, exactly how it should be, so how would he take this—

"Did you fall in? I mean, I know the shrimp last night wasn't the greatest. Maybe I should call Maguire, see if anyone else has had a problem? But these movers are already bringing in stuff, so—*No, don't put that there!*" he shouted, and Lila knew she had to face the music before the movers scratched their perfect new hardwood floors.

Slowly, she dropped the stick into the trash and stepped out, her thoughts on what she'd just seen, how it could be wrong, but then she'd missed her period, and she'd never missed her period before, and . . .

Deep breath. Long, deep breath.

"Hey," Charlie said, eyeing her. "Ready to bring in some boxes?"

"Actually." Lila fumbled with her ponytail, then wrung out her hands, then placed them on her hips. "I . . . well, I don't think I should be moving any boxes."

His eyebrows drew in. "Feeling sick? I knew you looked off last night. Stomach bug?"

She laughed. "Well, that's one way to put it."

"Huh? You're not making sense here, and these movers are about to ruin my new floor."

A slow grin spread across her face. "*Your* new floors?"

"Well, yeah, mine. Ours. Mine." He laughed, then took her hand and pulled. "Now let's get to those boxes."

"Wait." Charlie paused, and Lila ran her hands over her face. "I can't move boxes, because see, I think I might be . . . a little on the pregnant side. Okay, a lot on the pregnant side, and they say you shouldn't lift heavy things, and maybe that's just an old wives' tales, but I don't really know all the dos and don'ts yet. Because I'm an animal doctor, not a human doctor. And I know this is poor timing, and we've just taken on two new businesses, and it's . . . well, I don't even know how this happened! Damn pill not working." Lila stomped her foot, then peered back up at her husband. "It's . . . I . . ."

And then Charlie swept her into his arms, laughter booming out of his chest. "We're having a baby?"

"Yes, I think so. Does this mean you're happy?"

"We're having a baby!" he screamed, at the very moment that Zac and Brady appeared.

"Ah, damn," Zac said. "Well there went my hope of being the favorite son by giving Mama a new baby this year." Then he grinned and Sophie and Audrey rushed in, hugging Lila close.

"When did you find out?" they all asked.

"Just now."

The women all squealed and set into to talking about baby rooms and baby clothes and baby showers. And as Charlie took her hand and kissed her palm, and her gaze took in their excited family and friends, she knew Crestler's Key would forever be her safe haven.

Her home.

ABOUT THE AUTHOR

Melissa West writes heartfelt Southern romance and teen sci-fi romance, all with lots of kissing. Because who doesn't like kissing? She lives outside of Atlanta, Georgia, with her husband and two daughters and spends most of her time writing, reading, or fueling her coffee addiction.

Connect with Melissa at www.melissawestauthor.com or on Twitter @MB_West.

MELISSA WEST

FIGHTING LOVE

THE LITTLETON BROTHERS